**"You're a dangerous man,
M. J. Connover."**

Mick's smile stretched. "I'm a pussycat, Stevie. Will you go out with me tonight?"

"No," Stevie said softly. She didn't stop to think about it. She *couldn't* stop to think about it.

"Why?" Mick's eyes revealed nothing beyond polite curiosity.

"It would be too... complicated."

"Really?" His head tilted slightly. "What you see is what you get. Do you know something I don't?"

Uncomfortable, Stevie turned to the window. "Never mind. You wouldn't understand."

Mick came up beside her, looking out the window. His shoulder brushed hers, and he heard her indrawn breath. He inhaled her scent with every breath, and thoughts he didn't dare speak came and went in his mind. "I probably should warn you. I don't deal with rejection very well...."

Courtney Ryan

Courtney Ryan first began writing for Second Chance at Love in 1985 and, she says, has been happily ignoring housework ever since. "My adorable children truly appreciate the occasional ironed shirt. My adorable husband has long since learned to iron his own shirts."

Courtney's favorite things include "uneventful airplane flights, Cary Grant movies, rainy afternoons, feather pillows, and fearless brown-eyed schnauzer dogs. Ah, yes, and skiing the greatest snow on earth—in Utah, naturally." She wants to thank Second Chance at Love readers who have taken the time to write to her. "Their comments and encouragement are sincerely appreciated."

Dear Reader:

Romance is handled with a light touch by this month's witty and insightful authors. Courtney Ryan, author of *Cody's Gypsy* (#438) which so many of you loved, has outdone herself—again—in *Ten to Midnight* (#468). And for skilled new Second Chance at Love author Deanna Lindon, not even the sky's the limit in *Air Dancer* (#469).

It's amazing, but true. In *Ten to Midnight* (#468), Courtney Ryan has crafted a plot, hero, and heroine as entertaining as her many others over the years. When Stevie Knight, the owner of—and force behind—a company that specializes in unforgettable events, is hired to kidnap a groom-to-be, it's just another day at the office for her. So when her partner delivers a blindfolded and bewildered M. J. Connover to Stevie's limo, she takes off for the bachelor party that awaits. Another mission accomplished it seems, but Stevie doesn't realize she has the wrong Connover. Happily a hostage of the seductive voice and entertaining antics of his kidnapper, Mick doesn't say a thing. If only he could see the face behind the voice, and the mouth that surprises him with a good-bye kiss before he's dumped on the corner. Though she does her best to remain undiscovered, Stevie inevitably surrenders to Mick's disarming ways. But there's still one hurdle Stevie has to overcome before she'll be Mick's willing captive forever...

Gypsy Gallagher is an adventurous soul whose truly happy moments are those she spends airborne. An acknowledged flying ace, clear weather and a free schedule are her only requisites for the perfect day. Of course, her life hasn't always been that simple. But tragedy's place is in the past; Gypsy is more interested in the future. Big-time journalist Keane McCready is interested in the future, too—ideally a future with Gypsy. Assigned to cover her for his magazine, Keane is taken with this fiery spirit full of surprises. Gypsy's only interest, however, is in getting rid of him. Not only does Keane stir disturbing images of the past, he's wreaking havoc on the present. She refuses to be grounded by any man, this handsome reporter included. But Keane's determined to exorcise the past and eliminate the barrier that keeps him from his *Air Dancer* (#469).

Also from Berkley this month is new author Teresa Medeiros. In *Lady of Conquest*, we're taken back to ancient Ireland and the time of the Fianna, led by Conn of the Hundred Battles and Gelina Ò Monaghan, who wields a sword called Vengeance. Despoiler of Gelina's family, Conn takes her in when she has no one. Not yet a woman, Gelina still is able to stand alone against Ireland's mightiest warriors; she has a will of steel until it is weakened by her passion for the one man she hates most. Their forbidden love becomes a personal war fought with swords and embraces, promises and betrayal. In the tradition of *Lion of Ireland*, *Lady of Conquest* is a beautifully written historical novel that will stay with you for a long time to come...

The sizzling *New York Times* bestseller, *The Duchess of Windsor* by Charles Higham, is now a Charter paperback. The world has held the Duchess of Windsor—Mrs. Wallis Simpson—in endless fascination. But until now, the world hasn't heard much of what there is to know. Her power over Edward VIII, who gave up his throne for her . . . her fairy-tale rise to royalty . . . her ruthless power schemes ... her unique seductive bedroom practices ... her notorious Nazi connections. Fully documented from exclusive sources, *The Duchess of Windsor* unveils the secret life of one of the most talked-about women of the century. "Fascinating!" *USA Today.* "A shocker!" *Cosmopolitan.* Don't miss it!

Wildflower, by Jill Marie Landis, author of the spectacular novel *Sunflower,* is truly a fabulous read. Meet Dani, a spirited beauty, who, dressed as a man, dupes unwanted attackers and survives the untamed Rocky Mountain wilderness of 1830. But her heart holds passionate dreams and unspoken desires. And meet Troy, a darkly handsome explorer who kidnaps Dani on a lark, and is himself captivated by her beauty and unwavering spirit. From the great peaks of the West to the lush seclusion of a Caribbean jungle, Dani and Troy discover the deepest treasures of the heart.

August is a great month for romance. I can almost promise you September will be even better! Until then, happy reading!

Hillary Cige

Hillary Cige, Editor
SECOND CHANCE AT LOVE
The Berkley Publishing Group
200 Madison Avenue
New York, NY 10016

SECOND CHANCE AT LOVE™

COURTNEY RYAN
TEN TO MIDNIGHT

B

BERKLEY BOOKS, NEW YORK

TEN TO MIDNIGHT

First edition published August 1989

ISBN: 0-425-11707-3

Second Chance at Love books are published by
The Berkley Publishing Group
200 Madison Avenue, New York, NY 10016

Printed in the United States of America

10 9 8 7 6 5 4 3 2 1

Chapter

1

9:50 P.M.

THEY WERE RUNNING BEHIND. The original plan
had called for the kidnapping to take place at
9:45 P.M. Unfortunately, there was a bit of a
problem with the disguises. The driver of the getaway car—actually, getaway limousine—had
forgotten to rent the shiny black boots that com-
pleted the chauffeur's uniform. Pink and white
Reeboks were substituted. Not a great catas-
trophe, since the chauffeur's feet were unlikely to
be noticed by anyone. The real problem came
with the policeman's trousers. You see, in this
particular kidnapping, the policeman played a
significant role.

"The damn zipper won't stay up," the police-

1

man complained. "Haven't you got a safety pin or something?"

The chauffeur guided the limousine along the brick-paved driveway that scalloped the Connover estate. There were cars parked on either side as far as the eye could see: a Mercedes and Porsche parade. Moonlight picked out gleaming silver and gold hubcaps. The rich did enjoy their hubcaps.

"I told you, I haven't got a safety pin," the chauffeur replied. "You should have thought of that before you left home."

"Gosh, Mommy. I'm sorry."

"Touchy tonight, aren't we? Just keep your hand over it."

"Oh, that will look just dandy, won't it? Where're my handcuffs?"

"On the seat there."

"Damn it, where's my hat? I had it just a—"

The chauffeur sighed. "Backseat. Will you please relax? It's not like we've never done this before."

"I've never had a broken zipper before. You know how I feel about getting into my roles. How can I be convincing as a dedicated public servant with my fly hanging... Wait. There. I think I've got it. If I don't breathe, I'll be fine."

"Good. Wonderful. Don't breathe." The limousine pulled smoothly to a halt in front of the Connover mansion. Built high in the hills overlooking San Diego, the multi-peaked roof etched a miniature skyline against the starlit sky. Party sounds drifted on the night wind: an elegant murmur. "Here we go, then. Have you got everything?"

"Everything but oxygen." The policeman whistled softly, gazing at the brick palace nestled in the mountainside. "Will you look at this place? Cozy little cottage, isn't it?"

"If you're into mausoleums, it's great. Wait a minute, you've pinned your badge upside down... There. You know, you don't look half bad in that uniform. If you ever decide to give up kidnapping, you might consider police work."

"Now *there's* a thought."

Mick Connover was not having a good time.

It didn't show on his face. He was on his best behavior tonight, dancing and chatting and mingling with grim determination. It was the least he could do for his older brother, endure this pre-wedding party hysteria with a semblance of good humor. In less than twenty-four hours, Marshall would be a married man. Mick stood in admiration of anyone prepared to take that oh-so-final step. He could certainly do his part by smiling his way through this formal evening. Providing the muscles in his cheeks didn't seize up.

Besides, he had the bachelor party to look forward to later. He wasn't sure what Marshall's friends had planned, but it had to be more entertaining than nibbling on fish eggs and making small talk with two hundred strangers.

Privately, Mick promised himself something

more down-to-earth for his own pre-nuptial brouhaha, should that happy day ever arrive. None of this dash and splash his family was so fond of. A nice little clambake on the beach, maybe, or beer and pretzels down at Webb's Bar & Grill. He tried to visualize his dainty mother hefting a foaming mug in a toast to the bride and groom. The mind boggled.

"Michael James! How good to see you."

Mick turned his attention to the silver-haired woman patting his arm. She was vaguely familiar, though he couldn't recall a name. A distant relative, more than likely. No one else would dare call him Michael James. "How are you?" he said politely. "How very good to see you again. You're looking lovely."

She smiled, displaying a smudge of cranberry-red lipstick on her front tooth. "So sweet. Why didn't I see you in the reception line earlier?"

Probably because I was having a beer in the kitchen. "Oh, I was around. Are you enjoying yourself?"

"Very much. Dinner was superb, and this orchestra is ... well, there are no words. I'm so pleased for your brother, darling. Tamara's a lovely, lovely girl. Your parents must be thrilled."

"Tickled pink," Mick said. "And now if you'll excuse me—"

"By the way, have you seen Cherise tonight?"

"I don't believe I have." Mick had no idea who Cherise was.

"Oh, you won't recognize my little girl. Those few extra pounds simply melted away, just as I told her they would. Nothing but baby fat."

"Isn't that nice? I'll keep an eye out for her. And now if you'll excuse me—"

"Pardon me, Mr. Connover." One of the waiters tapped him on the shoulder. "You have a visitor."

Mick looked at the crush of bodies on the dance floor. "I noticed."

"No, sir." The waiter glanced nervously over his shoulder. "This visitor is ... different. He's waiting for you in the entry hall."

His curiosity piqued, Mick made his excuses to Cherise's fond mother for a third time. He dodged another group of relatives, skirted the buffet table, and slipped through the French doors that led to the main hall. He also took the opportunity to loosen the bow tie that was choking him.

And then he stopped dead in his tracks, his dress shoes skidding on the marble floor. A policeman stood in the shadow of his mother's beloved African palm, a policeman in full uniform, complete with gun and handcuffs and a Clint Eastwood scowl.

The waiter was right. This visitor was different.

"I was told you were looking for me," Mick said slowly, keeping a wary eye on the gun. Had he done anything illegal lately? No, not since he'd gone fishing without a license last April.

Surely they couldn't have found out about that?

"M. J. Connover?"

The guy even talked like a Clint Eastwood clone. Raspy. Expressionless. "In person," Mick replied. "What can I do for you?"

"I'm Officer Morgan. I'm afraid I have to put you under arrest, sir."

"What?"

"Traffic violation. Apparently you've ignored the summons you received."

"What summons? I never received any summons!"

"I'm afraid you'll have to take that up with the judge, sir. You'll have to come with me. You have the right to remain silent . . ."

Mick had never been arrested before. It was an experience he could have lived without. Officer Morgan read him his rights in a bored monotone, then cuffed his hands behind his back.

"You've got to be kidding," Mick said incredulously. "Handcuffs? For a traffic violation?"

"Regulation, sir."

He was handcuffed like a common criminal— and all because of a few dozen parking tickets he'd collected over the past few months. Mick truly didn't recall receiving any summons. He'd fully intended to pay the damn tickets. He always did, sooner or later.

Thankfully, there was no one nearby to witness his arrest. The butler had made himself scarce. Likewise the nervous waiter. Mick had no desire to disrupt his brother's celebration with this unexpected development. With any luck, he could pay whatever fines he owed and make it back to the party before anyone noticed his absence.

Officer Morgan clapped a firm hand on Mick's arm and escorted him out the front door and down the white marble steps that led to the courtyard. The elaborately sculptured grounds were blazing with floodlights, illuminating majestic palm trees, manicured flower gardens, and sparkling fountains. The courtyard itself was circled with lush green hedges trimmed in the shape of birds—one of his mother's inspirations.

"Nice night to be arrested," Mick said laconically. He noticed a dark gray limousine with smoked-glass windows idling in the courtyard, but there was no sign of Officer Morgan's squad car. "So where's the old black-and-white? Hey, can we drive with the siren going and the lights flashing? I've always wanted to do that."

Officer Morgan was not amused. "Why do I always get the comedians? Just come with me, please."

"You know, you do a great Clint Eastwood impersonation. Has anyone ever told you that?"

The policeman's thin lips twisted in what might or might not have been the flicker of a smile. "I'm just doing my job, pal. Here we are."

They stopped beside the gray limousine. Baffled, Mick looked from Officer Morgan to the car and back again. "You arrest a man for parking violations and transport him in a limo? What does a bank robber get, a Lear jet?"

The policeman opened the rear door. Mick had a brief glimpse of the lush gray interior before a blindfold was suddenly slipped over his eyes. "Hey, what the hell—"

"Welcome to your bachelor party," Officer Morgan said. "I now leave you in Stevie's capable hands. Enjoy, buddy."

Mick was blind, bewildered and temporarily mute. With a little help from Officer Morgan, he took a nosedive into the backseat of the limousine. "Hold it," he managed finally, his voice muffled against the soft leather. "You've got your wires crossed, guys. I'm not the—"

The car door clicked shut. Mick heard two soft raps on the roof, a signal to move. The limousine pulled forward, dark and silent. Mick heaved himself upright in the seat, cracking his knee against something hard. "Ouch! What the hell was that?"

"The bar," a female voice said. "You hit your knee on the edge of the bar. Are you all right?"

Oh, yes. That was unmistakably a woman's voice. Mick sat quite still, suddenly oblivious to the dull throbbing in his knee. Perhaps being kidnapped, blindfolded and handcuffed made him more sensitive to sound, but never in his life had he heard such a sweet-flowing, seductive voice. So soft and husky, the faintest trace of a dreamy southern accent.

"What was the question?" he said.

A soft chuckle. "Are you all right? I specialize in painless abductions, believe it or not."

Mick's thoughts were scrambled. Jumping. "Painless?"

"Don't worry. I'll make it up to you. I've not had a single complaint from any of my kidnap victims."

"I can believe that." Mick cleared his throat. "You're . . . Steve?"

"Stevie. Why don't you sit back and relax, Mr. Connover? You have a big night ahead of you."

Stephanie Elizabeth Knight was having a very good time.

She loved driving the limousine. It gave her quite a heady feeling, maneuvering the powerful car down the unpredictable mountain roads. Not a single tree did she sideswipe. Not one scrubby bush did she flatten. It was quite an achievement, considering the meager little strip of asphalt she had to work with.

The scenery wasn't bad, either. The city of San Diego sparkled below her like diamond dust on black velvet. Moonlight spilled over the quiet water in the bay, shivering with the gentle tide. She took a deep breath, trying to memorize the dreamy vista, letting the tranquility drift through her. San Diego had been her home for nearly seven years, yet still it managed to take her by surprise.

The rearview mirror also provided a nice bit of scenery. Tonight's victim was quite attractive, blindfold and all. Marshall John Connover had Mel Gibson's jaw and Don Johnson's lips. It was a potent combination. His hair was the color of dark honey, straight and thick and ribbon-shiny. It was also endearingly dishevelled, spilling over the blindfold in a heavy tangle. No wonder. Morgan had been less than gentle when he had tossed him into the backseat. She would have to have a word with him about his tough guy persona. Morgan always tended to go overboard with his character interpretations.

From the backseat: "You don't sound like a Stevie. Is that an alias? I suppose most kidnappers use an alias."

She smiled. "It's a nickname. My friends and my hostages call me Stevie. My real name doesn't suit me at all."

"I don't suppose you'd tell me your real—"

"Of course not," Stevie said promptly, swerving to avoid a frantic squirrel in the road. "I'm not about to tell you my real name. Don't you know anything about kidnapping etiquette?"

"Sorry," Mick replied. "It's my first time, you know. I'm really not sure what to expect."

"Then let me enlighten you, Mr. Connover. Since this is your last night as a free man—so to speak—your friends wanted to make sure it was unforgettable. My company specializes in unforgettable events."

Mick nodded. "You do have a unique way of doing business." His nose was itching. He tipped his head, trying to scratch it against the seat. "You must be very successful."

"Thank you. I hope Morgan wasn't too rough on you."

"Morgan?" Mick frowned beneath the blindfold. "Oh . . . the policeman."

"Actually he's my partner. He's also a part-time actor. He takes his roles very seriously."

"I noticed. Where did he disappear to?"

"Oh, his car was parked at the bottom of your parents' drive," Stevie said. "He had another little job to do tonight."

"Tell him from me that he watches too many Clint Eastwood movies. Other than that, he was very authentic. This evening has already been truly unforgettable."

"As they say, 'You ain't seen nothin' yet.'" Stevie pressed a button on the dashboard. Soft piano music began filtering through the built-in stereo speakers. "I was told you're very fond of this particular artist. Do you know this tape?"

Mick was temporarily silenced with an attack of conscience. Obviously Marshall's friends had arranged this unorthodox prelude to his bachelor party. It was all intended for the unsuspecting groom-to-be . . . the kidnapping, the limousine, the piano music. And Stevie.

If he was any sort of a man, he would put an end to the charade immediately. He would tell Stevie she had kidnapped the wrong M. J. Connover. He would go back to the dinner party and nibble on more caviar and try not to slip into a coma out of sheer boredom.

That was certainly what he ought to do.

"You're very quiet, Mr. Connover," Stevie said.

Mr. Connover. Mick loved the way she said his name, rolling it around her tongue with that delicate southern drawl. Mr. Connover . . .

"Call me Marshall," he said, passing a silent apology to his brother.

"Marshall it is." Stevie had never found a rearview mirror quite so fascinating. Beneath the blindfold, his lips were curved in a wry, elusive smile. She wondered what color his eyes were.

She turned her attention back to her driving barely in time to negotiate a hairpin curve. She turned the wheel sharply, tires swerving, spitting gravel on the soft shoulder of the road. "Sorry about that," she muttered. "It got away from me for a second."

"Quite all right." Mick grinned, enjoying himself more and more. "Although I'd probably find the ride more interesting if I could see where we were going. What are the chances of taking this blindfold off?"

"Zero to none," Stevie said. "Anonymity is an important part of my work. The fewer people who recognize me, the better I can serve my clientele."

"Then you actually do kidnap people for a living? Are you in the yellow pages?"

"Not under kidnappers." Her words were arrhythmic because of the underlying laughter. "We also specialize in elaborate practical jokes, unforgettable birthday, anniversary and retirement celebrations... The list is endless."

He broke into a full-fledged charmer of a smile with enough heat to fog the rearview mirror. "And wild bachelor parties?"

"We did have a hand in your bachelor party," Stevie confessed, trying to ignore that smile. Heaven knew it was no simple thing to ignore. "At least Morgan did, which is another reason I prefer to remain anonymous. He's famous—or rather, infamous—for his bachelor parties, and good taste is no object."

"A man after my own heart," Mick commented. "I can hardly wait."

"Unfortunately you'll have to," Stevie said cheerfully. "According to the master plan, I'm to keep you under lock and key until midnight."

"What happens at midnight?"

"Ah, that's for me to know and for you to find out... at midnight." Stevie turned the limousine onto the frontage road that would eventually take them into San Diego. "Right now I think I'll treat you to A Taste of Heaven."

"Beg pardon?" Mick did his damnedest to sound nonchalant—and failed miserably.

"A Taste of Heaven. Don't tell me you've never heard of it?"

"I've heard of it," he muttered. "I've just never... tasted it."

"You poor deprived man. That's what comes

from being in your tax bracket. You never get to experience the joys of fast food. I can see I'll have to educate you tonight."

"You've lost me." Mick sighed. "Not only have you handcuffed me and blindfolded me, but you've lost me."

Stevie grinned into the rearview mirror. Such an entrancing, woebegone curve on those masculine lips. "It's simple. I'm going to broaden your horizons, Marshall. No man should walk down the aisle until he's experienced A Taste of Heaven."

"I couldn't agree more," Mick said with heartfelt sincerity.

Fifteen minutes later, Stevie guided the limousine through the drive-in window of Heavenly Hash. The hamburgers were so-so, she told her captive, but the chocolate-covered, triple-scoop ice-cream cones were to die for.

"Which is probably why they call them A Taste of Heaven," Mick guessed. And sighed. He wasn't quite sure what he had been anticipating, but this was something of a letdown.

"Such a smart man. There are twenty-two flavors. Would you like me to read them to you?"

"That could take a while. Aren't you afraid the attendant will think our little arrangement is kind of suspicious?"

"You mean the blindfold and handcuffs? Feeling a bit conspicuous, are you? The windows are tinted. He can't see a thing. Would you like to try the Passion Fruit flavor? Very appropriate for a man about to be married."

Soon, Mick promised himself. He would tell her the truth very soon. Right after the ice cream. "Passion Fruit sounds fine."

Stevie parked the limousine at the far end of the lot, near the Heavenly Hash dumpster painted with glow-in-the-dark halos. Then she joined her hostage in the backseat, armed with a dozen napkins and a Passion Fruit Taste of Heaven.

"What are you doing?" Mick asked, feeling her tuck something into the collar of his dress shirt.

"It's a napkin," Stevie said. "You need a bib if I'm going to feed you an ice-cream cone. These things are incredibly messy."

"I'm not going to sit here while you feed me. If you'll take off these handcuffs—"

"No way, José. Open up."

"This is so damned embarrassing. How about the blindfold? Take off the blindfold so I can see what I'm eating."

"It's dripping all over my hand." Stevie licked the dribble of ice cream off her fingers. "Mmmm . . . so good. I've never had Passion Fruit before. If you don't be a good boy and let me feed you, I'm going to eat the whole thing myself."

"Something tells me you would." Mick felt the startling coldness touch his lips; instinctively his tongue flicked out and he tasted sweet chocolate and a refreshing, fruit-flavored ice cream. "This is a little spooky. I usually don't eat what I can't see."

"But it's good, isn't it?" Stevie prompted softly, smiling at him. Or rather, smiling at the rueful, little-boy expression on his expressive lips. She'd never seen a mouth quite like his. Tender, whimsical, expressive... and sensual, even with ice cream smeared at the corners. The very fabric of sweet, wild fantasies. Again, she wondered what his eyes looked like beneath that blindfold. "Actually, the ice cream should taste even better this way. When you lose the sense of sight and touch, the other senses grow that much stronger."

Mick could well believe it. At the moment, his senses were focused on something far more intriguing than Passion Fruit. He was tantalized by Stevie's nearness. He could smell her perfume, an unusual, hypnotic blend of lilac and musk. And her sensual voice surrounded him in the close confines of the car, an erotic physical presence. This night felt wonderful. This moment felt wonderful. "Can I ask you something?"

She watched him licking the ice-cream cone in slow, sensual motion, and felt a sudden surprising shiver of awareness deep in the core of her abdomen. The blood that gathered in her cheeks rushed hot and pounding into her arms, her fingers, enough heat to make Passion Fruit soup. Embarrassed, she tried to compose her expression, grateful he couldn't see her face. "Ask away," she said.

"What do you look like?" Mick was desperate to know. Her voice was a miracle. She had humor, intelligence, and an innate sensuality. She was feminine and independent. He felt he knew all this, but he had absolutely no idea what she looked like. It was driving him crazy. "If you won't take off the blindfold, at least give me a general description. My curiosity is killing me."

Stevie smiled to herself. With her free hand, she took off the chauffeur's cap she had been wearing, shaking a satin-soft cloud of black hair around her shoulders. "All right," she said mischievously. "I suppose it won't do any harm. I have red hair. At school everyone used to call me carrot-top."

"Long hair?"

"Short."

"Straight?"

"Curly. And freckles," she added on a sudden inspiration. Her flawless olive skin was naturally sun-kissed, gifting her with a perpetual tan regardless of the amount of time she spent outdoors. "I suffer from the redhead's curse—pale skin and an epidemic of freckles."

Mick frowned. "You don't *sound* like a redhead," he said.

"And what do redheads sound like?" Stevie asked.

"Well . . . I don't know. What about your eyes? Let me guess." He couldn't be wrong on this one. She had to have blue eyes, he felt it in his bones. "They're blue, right?"

"Nope," Stevie replied, staring at him with diamond-bright blue eyes. "Hazel. They look kind of green when I wear green, brown when I wear brown." She wiped at a dribble of ice cream on his chin with a corner of a napkin. "Anything else you'd like to know?"

"How tall are you?"

Stevie was five-foot two. Whenever she drove the limousine, she sat on a pillow. "I'll give you a hint," she said. "When they weren't calling me carrot-top in school, they were calling me bean-pole."

"Tall?"

"Very." It was getting nearly impossible to stifle the laughter. She disguised it as a cough. "And now if your curiosity is satisfied, we should be leaving. It's nearly midnight."

"And the limo turns into a pumpkin at midnight?"

"No," Stevie said, wrapping the remains of the dripping ice-cream cone in a napkin. "At the stroke of midnight, it is officially June fifteenth. Your wedding day, in case you've forgotten." Stevie's smile faltered suddenly. His wedding day. For a few minutes she'd been the one who'd forgotten that little item. Marshall Connover with the beautifully chiseled lips and slow, sexy smile was about to be married. Stevie shook her head, making a small sound of denial, of self-derision. She dragged her eyes and her thoughts away from him, firmly shoving the chauffeur's cap back on her head. "Besides, your bachelor party awaits you. The drunken revelry is scheduled to begin at midnight. The guest of honor can't be late."

"I'm not—" Mick heard the car door open and close, realized she'd gone. "I'm not the guest of honor," he said to the empty car. "My name is Mick. My brother Marshall is the guest of honor." There. That wasn't hard. Now all he had to do was repeat it when she got back in the car.

Stevie threw the ice-cream cone into the dumpster, then slipped into the driver's seat of the limousine. "It's a quarter till twelve," she said, glancing at her watch. "We ought to just make it."

"*We* will," Mick muttered in a barely audible voice. "Poor ol' Marshall won't."

The engine purred to life. "What's that?"

"Nothing."

Mick practiced silently as they drove. *I'm sorry I didn't tell you sooner. I should have. If I hadn't been having such a good time, I would have . . .*

They pulled up in front of the Hyatt Regency Hotel at five minutes to twelve. Stevie left the car idling, opened the passenger door and helped her hostage to his feet. He stumbled on the curb and they both nearly went down.

"Sorry," Stevie said gruffly.

"You don't sound tall."

"Well, I am. Very." Hand on his arm, she guided him to the sidewalk in front of the hotel. Passersby stopped and stared. Stevie was quite oblivious to the commotion they caused. She had ceased to concern herself with other people's opinions long ago. "Here we are," she said cheerfully. "You've been delivered safe and sound. I won't be responsible for your condition after the bachelor party, however."

"Here we are *where*?" Mick asked, stalling for time.

"Hyatt Regency. Your friends rented the Grand Ballroom."

"No, they didn't."

Stevie looked at him curiously. "Of course they did. I was here earlier. I saw the decorations and a six-foot high cardboard cake. Heaven only knows what Morgan filled it with."

"They aren't my friends," Mick said. "I'm not Marshall. I'm his brother, Mick." There, it was done. No grace, no tact, but it was done.

"What are you talking about?" Stevie asked, bewildered. "You told me you were M. J. Connover. You told Morgan you were M. J. Connover."

"I *am* M. J. Connover," he said. "Michael James. Mick to my friends and captors. My older brother is the one getting married tomorrow—Marshall John Connover. I take it you never saw a picture of him when you were hired?"

"But we did! Your friends—his friends—showed us a Polaroid. It wasn't a very good picture, but it certainly looked like you. Brown hair, about six feet tall . . ."

"Stevie, Marshall has brown hair, too. And we're both exactly six feet tall."

Silence. Stevie tried to collect her scattered wits.

"You'd better send a cab for Marshall," Mick suggested wryly.

She felt a smile tugging at her lips. She ought to be absolutely furious, but she wasn't. There was a part of her, a small, secret part that was experiencing a wave of guilty relief. How strange. Married or single, this man was a crown prince of the upper class. And Stevie Knight was allergic to heights.

"Why did you do it?" she asked finally. "Why didn't you tell me we had the wrong man?"

The corners of his mouth tilted in a beguiling grin. "I was having a good time."

Stevie laughed to herself, shaking her head. "I was having a good time," she mimicked softly. "You're right. I'd better send a cab for Marshall. But first . . ."

"The handcuffs?" Mick asked hopefully.

"In a minute." Stevie's lips were slightly parted, and the flush in her cheeks was back. She had made a decision in the last three seconds, based on pure, mischievous impulse. As were most of her decisions. Life was too short for arduous deliberation.

Her gentle fingers touched his jaw, her thumb brushing his lower lip. She barely registered his sudden, sharp intake of breath. "M. J. Connover," she said huskily, "you've been a very nice hostage and you have the most incredibly sexy mouth I have ever seen in my life."

Her smile widened. She rose up on tiptoe, her hat fell off, and she kissed him.

Mick was stunned. Her kiss was like an erotic whisper against his lips, incredibly soft and warm. She was scented of lilacs and the fresh night air, and her palm was hot against his cheek. He made a small, involuntary groan deep in his throat, then his lips opened under hers and he was returning her kiss with heart-stopping intensity, his pulse hammering in his throat, his veins flooding with electric heat.

No one had ever moved him like this, so quickly, so effortlessly. He couldn't touch her. He couldn't see her. Another thirty seconds of this and he would be completely insane.

Stevie broke away, breathing erratically, blue eyes softly unfocused. "Well, now I know," she whispered. Her voice had an odd, hoarse tone. She pushed her trembling fingers into her pocket and brought forth a small metal key. She reached around his back, pressing the key into his hand. "You'll have to find someone to unlock the handcuffs," she said. "We have quite an audience. You shouldn't have too much trouble."

"Wait a minute—"

"I really have to go, or Marshall won't make it to his party. Good-bye, M. J. Connover. It's been an unforgettable evening."

"You're going to leave me standing here? Like this?" He heard the car door slam. "Dammit, at least take off the blindfold! I don't even know what you look like!"

Stevie stuck her head out the window. "I told you. Carrot-top. Bean-pole. Could someone please help this poor man? He's been kidnapped."

The limousine pulled away from the curb. M. J. Connover said a very bad word.

Chapter
2

THE BRIDE WAS RADIANT. The groom was a bit pale. The best man had faint red welts on his wrists.

The wedding was held in the formal garden at the rear of the Connover estate, with the assembled company protected from the afternoon sunlight by a huge silver marquee. Mick was deeply grateful for the shade. He was still suffering the aftereffects of the bachelor party. Light hurt. Sound hurt. Movement hurt. He remained stonestill throughout the ceremony, more out of desperation than reverence. Silently he repeated his own personal vows along with his brother's. *I, Michael James Connover, do promise and covenant never to touch another drop of liquor as long as I shall live . . .*

The bachelor party had been quite an experience. Marshall had arrived some thirty minutes late, claiming to have been abducted from his parents' home by a six-foot gorilla.

Mick remembered Stevie's description of herself as a bean pole. Could that gorilla possibly have been...? "Did you hear her voice?" he asked.

Marshall looked at him as if he were crazy. "*Her* voice? What makes you think it was a woman?"

"Well, was it?"

"I really don't know how to tell the difference with gorillas," Marshall said. "But if it was a woman, she had a voice like Clint Eastwood and a grip like Rambo. Why are you wearing that weird hat?"

Mick touched the chauffeur's cap on his head. He'd picked it up off the sidewalk after a hesitant doorman had finally been persuaded to unlock the handcuffs. "What do you mean, weird? This hat is a keepsake. It belongs to a kidnapper who smells like lilacs."

Marshall smiled. "Of course it does."

"She kissed me. She handcuffed me and blindfolded me and then she kissed me."

"Sure," Marshall said, unimpressed. "Why don't you switch to ginger ale for the rest of the night, little brother?"

Dispirited, Mick had proceeded straight to the bar. Two hours later, he could barely remember his own name—but he couldn't forget the sound of Stevie's voice. If only he had a face to put with that voice. Or an address. Or a phone number, or a last name, or the license plate number of the limousine. *Anything.* He was feeling incredibly frustrated. Women who kidnapped men for a living and then cheerfully took advantage of them were hard to find in this world. Pleasantly drunk and melodramatic, Mick brooded over the loss of such a woman.

With the dawn came the cold reality of a hangover and an obvious course of action. He would find her. It was a simple matter of discovering which of Marshall's friends had hired Stevie to stage the kidnapping. *Voilà,* he would be reunited with his bewitching abductor—abductress?—and this time, Mick's hands wouldn't be cuffed behind his back.

Fortified with three extra-strength aspirin, Mick was able to perform the duties of best man with thin-lipped determination. After the ceremony, he was enfolded by the glossy merriment of the garden party. His heart wasn't in it, any more than his aching head. He substituted soft drinks for champagne. He danced with several women, nice slow dances that weren't likely to aggravate his tender condition. He had to smile when he noticed he wasn't the only pale-faced party animal walking on eggshells and sipping soda. Stevie had been right. Morgan certainly knew how to plan a bachelor party, if the condition of the survivors was anything to go by.

Two hours into the reception, Mick finally felt

capable of dealing with solid food. He wandered to the buffet table and picked idly at the fresh fruit. Not bad, but he wanted something more substantial. The lobster bisque smelled good. Kind of cheesy, with a hint of . . . lilacs?

Lilacs.

Stevie's perfume. He could smell her perfume. It was unmistakable, that sensual blend of lilac and musk. Mick spun on his heel in a quick half-circle, scanning the shifting crowd. He was surrounded by glittery fabrics and bright, white smiles and beautiful people with evenly tanned skin. Some he knew, many he didn't. As far as he could see, there wasn't a blazing redhead in the bunch, which didn't surprise him. He'd suspected that Stevie had been spinning a little fairy tale with her colorful description. He had no idea what she looked like, but he would bet his last two aspirin that she wasn't a carrot-top.

He concentrated on the blondes and brunettes, moving slowly through the crowd. He tried not to be too obvious. A little whiff here, a little whiff there. The scent of lilacs still hung faintly in the air, but he couldn't identify the source. His eye fell upon a curvaceous platinum blonde who looked like a fun-loving sort; he moved in closer for a perfume identification and nearly got his face slapped. Definitely not Stevie. Instinctively he knew she would be more inclined to throw a right hook than a coy little slap. The lady was an original.

After ten minutes of perfume sniffing, his eyes

were watering and the surrounding females had taken on a universal tutti-frutti fragrance. Feeling more than a little foolish, he retreated again to the buffet table. His bemused mother was waiting for him with a shrimp puff in hand.

"Do you mind telling me what you were doing?" she asked.

Mick sighed. It really wasn't his day. "I was socializing," he said. "You know . . . mingling. You always tell me I should mingle more at these events."

"Michael, dear, you were sniffing people," she said.

Mick patted his mother gently on her golden-blond head, so as not to muss her chignon. Rochelle Connover was famous for saying precisely what she thought, inspiring a great deal of admiration and fear in her family and friends. "Silly mother. Of course I wasn't sniffing people."

"You were."

"I wouldn't." He busied himself with the liver pâté. "Have you seen my new sister-in-law around? I haven't danced with her yet."

"I'm sure Tamara's devastated," his mother replied dryly. "Darling, don't do anything strange today. Please?"

Mick uncoiled his sweetest smile. "I'm tame."

"Dear heart, if you were tame, you would have gone into business with your father instead of opening that sporting goods store. You would live in a nice house instead of that adobe cottage thing of yours. You would drive a nice car instead of that rattletrap truck without doors."

"Jeep, mother. It's called a Jeep."

"And you wouldn't go around sniffing peo-ple." She took his arm, moving him away from the crowded buffet table. "I'm your mother. I want you to feel perfectly free to confide in me."

"There's this woman," Mick said promptly, his gaze bright and disarming. "She tied me up and fed me ice cream. She smelled like lilacs. I was trying to find her."

After a short pause she said, "Thank you for sharing that with me, dear. Everything is per-fectly clear now."

"Well, fine." Mick grinned and popped a cracker into his mouth. "Now you can relax and enjoy the party."

"I appreciate that," she said faintly, shaking her head as she turned away.

Mick's smile was short-lived. What on earth had he been thinking? One whiff of lilacs and he plunged into the crowd like a bloodhound on the scent. Heaven only knew what he would have done had he found a woman wearing lilac perfume . . . "Excuse me, but haven't I smelled you somewhere before?"

Idiot. Of course Stevie wouldn't be attending his brother's wedding. She wasn't a friend of the family. She didn't even know what Marshall looked like. She had been hired to help with the bachelor party, nothing more.

He would simply have to be patient. His first plan was still the best. He would talk with Marshall's friends, discover who had hired her, and arrange a proper introduction.

Patience, he thought, and sighed. It had never been one of his strengths.

"I have to tell you, I'm really not having a very good time. I think we ought to leave now."

"Be patient." Stevie tucked her arm through Morgan's, smiling up at him. "We can't leave yet. We just got here ten minutes ago."

"Don't tell me to be patient," Morgan replied, tugging at the knot in his tie. "I hate that word, I really do. Why on earth you had to drag me to this shindig, I'll never understand. Hell, I was here twice last night. The last thing I wanted to do was come back again today." He brightened suddenly, boyish creases cupping his smile. "Did I tell you one of the Connovers' guests fainted when she saw me in the King Kong suit? Well, she didn't actually hit the floor—"

"I'm so pleased."

"—but she did a great swoon. One of the waiters caught her. I do a great King Kong, if I do say so myself. Very primitive, with just a touch of vulnerability."

"Your talent is exceeded only by your humility," Stevie said.

Morgan grinned, accepting her remark with the imperturbability of a long-standing friendship. They had first met four years earlier when Stevie had rear-ended his car at a stoplight. Morgan had been deeply grateful; he'd despised the aged vehicle and had been waiting for years for the damn thing to break down, which it never did. By demolishing his car, Stevie had won his immediate friendship. Naturally, at first she had been wary of the young man who had given her a bone-crushing hug at the scene of the accident and professed himself to be eternally in her debt. It wasn't what she considered rational behavior. Four years later they were the best of friends as well as business partners, and Stevie still wasn't sure he was entirely rational.

"I'm glad you appreciate my talents," Morgan said affably. "Can we leave now? I have a hot date tonight. I need to clean the garbage out of my car."

Stevie propelled her reluctant date in the direction of the buffet table. Food always made Morgan happy. "We'll go soon," she promised. "Right now I need to find Tamara and give her my regards. I feel guilty enough about missing the wedding."

"Wasn't your fault," Morgan said, zeroing in on the shrimp puffs. "We had a flat tire."

"I still wish I'd been here." Stevie's eyes danced over strangers' faces. She tried to quell the excitement she was feeling. M. J. Connover, Mick to his friends and captors, was here somewhere. She chewed her bottom lip, wondering if he was near, wondering if he would recognize her. *Stupid*. Of course he wouldn't. He'd been blindfolded, and she'd lied through her teeth about her appearance. He'd never recognize her in a million years—which was exactly the way she wanted it.

"Do you see your friend anywhere?" Morgan asked.

"No . . . I don't see him."

Morgan's smile was bright in his sun-browned face. *"Him?* Why, sweetheart . . . I thought we were here to give our congratulations to your old college roommate. Am I missing something?"

"No." Stevie's cheeks burned. "I meant *her*. Tamara and I were very good friends when we went to Vassar, I told you that. She's very nice, very personable—"

"You don't have to sell her to me," Morgan said cheerfully. "She's the one who recommended us for the job last night, and we made a bundle on it. As far as I'm concerned, she's a jewel."

"You're such a sensitive man," Stevie said sweetly. "I'm so fortunate to . . ."

Suddenly she stilled, her hand in the air, her mouth open in surprise. He was there, just across the table. Mick Connover, with the beautiful mouth and the strong, square jaw. She couldn't stop the tiny gasp that escaped her at the sight of this man.

His eyes were brown—a rich, chocolate brown with sun-colored sparkles. They were gentle with humor, compelling with heart-stopping sensuality. For several seconds she lost herself in those eyes . . . until she realized they were focused directly on her. Searching. Widening.

He knew her.

She dropped her eyes. She couldn't catch her breath, but oxygen was the least of her concerns. Frozen with surprise, ragged heartbeats spilling into her throat, she fought for a rational process of thought. Of course he didn't know her. He *couldn't* know her.

She found a smile and put it on and clung to Morgan like a vine. She had no choice now but to bluff her way through the next few minutes. There was no possible way Mick could identify her. None at all. She was perfectly safe.

If only she hadn't kissed him . . .

The moment he set eyes on her, he recognized her.

She was standing four feet away from him in a posture of frozen shock. Her hair was dark, ebony dark. It brushed her shoulders, moving slightly in the breeze. He could almost feel its baby-soft texture. She was petite, barely over five feet. His eyes swept over the slender lines of her body beneath her white silk sheath, the muscles tightening in his throat. She was luminous, perfect. Her olive skin was flawless, not a freckle to be seen. And her eyes . . . her eyes were incredible. They were the color of a warm summer sky, a pure, crystalline blue. *Blue.*

Stevie. She possessed not the slightest resemblance to the description she had given of herself, yet Mick knew. It was more than the lightning flash of awareness that had passed between them. It was more than a suspicion, more than the haunting fragrance of lilacs that again tantalized him. His heart had kicked into double time. His stomach was tight. His skin felt hot, prickling with a heightened sensitivity. His body recognized her with a frantic certainty.

She blinked once, then looked away. In the space of a heartbeat she had her features rearranged. She was smiling, touching her blond-haired escort lightly on the elbow. Composed and elegant. No one would ever guess this cool beauty was capable of taking advantage of a helpless kidnap victim.

"And thank heaven you were," Mick muttered, shouldering his way through the crowd, one eye on her glossy black head. *Don't move, Cinderella. I've found you again and I'm not about to lose you.*

Uncertainty and subliminal chemistry were playing havoc with Stevie's pulse rate. Since it wasn't in her nature to panic, she told herself her body's startled response to M. J. Connover was probably due to the awkwardness of the situation. It was unfortunate she had given in to the impulse to kiss him. It made the innocent act something of a strain.

Her fingers closed around Morgan's arm in a vise-grip. "Enough food," she said in a brittle voice. "If we don't circulate, we'll never find Tamara. If we don't find Tamara, you'll be late for your hot date."

"You do know how to motivate me," Morgan

murmured, stealing one last shrimp puff. "Wait, wait . . . I didn't try the chicken wings. You know how much I like sweet and sour—"

"Mercy me." Mick Connover stood in front of them, looking very much at ease in the gentle colors of sunset. "If it isn't the kissing bandit. I wonder if I should call security."

Stevie's smile faltered only briefly. She was expecting this. She simply wasn't . . . prepared. Her wary gaze connected with Mick's hypnotic, light-filled eyes. The air was filled with a strange intensity.

"I don't believe I know you," she said in a cool voice, complete with raised eyebrow. With some effort she relaxed her grip on Morgan's arm, lest he betray her with a yelp of pain. "Have we met?"

Smile lines teased the corners of Mick's soft brown eyes. She was very good, he thought. Almost—but not quite—convincing. "Not really," he answered. "At least, not officially." For the first time he took a good look at Stevie's escort. Immediately he recognized Dirty Harry's heavy-lidded green eyes. "And here's another old friend—my arresting officer. Enjoying the party, guys? You know, you just missed my mother. She would have loved to meet you."

Stevie looked at Morgan. He returned her gaze blankly, obviously at a loss for words. There would be no help from that direction, then. Morgan was terrible at improvisation. "We're enjoying the party very much," she said, "but I'm afraid you've confused us with someone else."

"There *is* no one else like you two," Mick returned easily. "By the way, I have your hat, Stevie. You dropped it last night when you kissed me."

Morgan choked. Stevie hit him on the back, her hand a small, knotted fist. "Are you all right, Morgan?"

"Something went down the wrong way," Morgan gasped.

"You should be more careful," Mick offered kindly.

Morgan stared at Stevie. "One of us certainly should. *Stephanie*, shouldn't we find Tamara now? It's getting late."

"Yes . . . of course." Stevie took a deep breath, desperate for every bit of it. Her gaze settled uncomfortably on Mick Connover's boyish, wayward smile. Had he shown any signs of uncertainty, she might have found it easier to cope with the situation. As it was, she felt completely off-balance, one faltering step behind her accustomed air of blithe self-confidence. How on earth had he recognized her?

"Oh, you're a friend of the bride," Mick said. "That surprises me. Tamara seems to be a very level-headed girl, very responsible. Does she know you kidnap people, Stevie?"

"I have no idea what you're talking about." He was studying her with curious intensity, and she found it terribly unnerving. "I don't think you're a well man," she added irritably. "You should consider professional counseling. Psychiatrists abound at gatherings like this. There's certain to be someone here who can give you the attention you need."

"I'm positive there is," Mick said peacefully. He was lost in her eyes. They were magnificent. They were filled with fire and spice, glittering with secrets. "I recognize your voice, you know," he went on, reaching out to tap her cheek with a teasing finger. "It's unmistakable, that sweet southern drawl."

"You couldn't possibly recognize my voice," Stevie said, lifting her chin, backing away from that gentle touch. "We've never spoken before."

"And you've never kidnapped me before?"

"Of course not." She tried to curb her southern accent, clipping her vowels and twanging her *r*'s. "I'd certainly remember you if I'd kidnapped you."

Mick's dark-eyed gaze smiled at her. "Don't talk like that. You sound like Pecos Bill. Just be yourself."

He was quite right. Stevie felt an answering smile fluttering to life deep within. She fought it. "I am myself, thank you very much."

Mick's expression fell into sad lines. "And you're *quite* sure you never kissed—"

"Never." She tugged impatiently on Morgan's hand. The man was a statue, his eyes focused thoughtfully on Mick Connover. "Coming, Morgan? Remember your hot date? The garbage in your car?"

"Vaguely." Morgan's lips tilted into a gently sardonic smile. "I've been a little distracted with all this talk about kidnapping and kissing. It kind of took me by surprise."

"It kind of took me by surprise, too," Mick murmured. "I can't say I didn't enjoy it, though. You certainly put your heart and soul into your work, Stevie."

Stevie turned to Morgan, shaking back her hair, neatly smoothing the white silk dress over her hips. When all else fails...fake it. "This poor man is deluded," she said simply. "I think the kindest thing we can do is ignore him. Shall we offer our congratulations to Tamara now?"

Mick burst out laughing. "Damn, but you're good. All right, I'll play your game...for now. You'll find Tamara and Marshall down by the gazebo, *Stephanie*. They're having some pictures taken." Then, as Stevie and Morgan turned away, "What? No fond farewells?"

Stevie glanced over her shoulder, still fighting that smile. "Farewell, Mr. Connover."

"Mistake," Mick replied in a creamy voice. "You're not supposed to know my name."

Touché. Her gaze locked with his, suspended in the whimsy and gentleness and sparkling golden light she saw in his eyes. She laughed suddenly, softly. "Lucky guess," she said.

Mick watched them walk away, an odd smile hovering about his lips. He had questions, dozens of them. Her name, for instance. Her address.

Her telephone number. Her relationship to Dirty Harry. The list went on and on.

Questions without answers . . . they bothered Michael James Connover. He had never been able to leave a crossword puzzle undone. He read the last chapter of a mystery novel first, and he always opened his Christmas presents early.

He gave himself twenty-four hours to find his answers.

"Well, that's another fine mess you've gotten us into," Morgan said.

They were walking down the cobblestone path that led to the gazebo and a lush, fragrant woods. The gardens surrounding them had been planted on seven descending levels, each overflowing with columbine, roses, asters, and dahlias. The sun dropped, blazing, in the west, and colored light washed over the fairy tale scene. It was an extravagant, poetic, and nostalgic atmosphere, completely wasted on Stevie Knight.

"I don't know what you're talking about," she said. "I wonder how much the Connovers spend on fertilizer?"

"Probably more than I spend on rent," Morgan said mildly, "and don't change the subject. Do you mind telling me what happened between you and Mr. Connover last night?"

"Nothing."

Morgan sighed and raised his eyes to heaven. "Forgive her," he murmured. "She's under a great deal of stress."

"All right. I kissed the man." Stevie shrugged, avoiding Morgan's eyes. "What can I say? I'm a little impulsive."

"No," he breathed, wide-eyed. "Really?"

"I certainly didn't expect him to recognize me today. When I kissed him, he was blindfolded. I never would have done it if I'd known he had X-ray vision. I repent. I'm sorry. End of story."

"Just like that?"

"Just like that."

Morgan threw her a look and a crooked, enigmatic smile. "Poor baby. What a lot you have to learn."

Chapter

3

MICK CONSIDERED HIMSELF A tactful and sensitive fellow. He knew that Marshall and Tamara were spending their wedding night at the Hilton Presidential Suite. Interrupting their first night as man and wife with a telephone call would have been rude and thoughtless. Instead, he waited until eight o'clock the following morning before telephoning them.

Marshall answered the phone after sixteen rings. His voice was less than welcoming. "Whoever you are, this better be important."

"Morning, big brother," Mick said cheerfully. "Have you looked outside? It's a beautiful day. Birdies, sunshine, all the good stuff."

A long pause. *"Mick?"*

"Of course it's Mick. Who else would call you on the Morning After?"

"I don't believe this. It's eight o'clock!"

"Time flies when you're having fun, doesn't it? Listen, may I talk to your wife, please?"

A longer pause. "Tamara? You called to talk to Tamara?"

"Yeah. Put her on, will you?"

"Dammit Mick, have you been drinking again?"

"Not a drop, I swear. I took my vows yesterday right along with you. From now on it's mineral water and ginger ale. Now let me talk to your wife, please. It's important." While he waited for Marshall to finish threatening him, Mick sat up in bed, kicking the covers to the floor. His "adobe cottage thing" was a golden cocoon on a summer morning. His bedroom faced east, and the tall windows were thrown open to the sun and the rocky green hills. This was Mick's sanctuary, his private breathing space that belonged just as much to the outdoors as the indoors. Completely relaxed, he warmed himself in the slanting sunlight until there was a pause in Marshall's tirade. "I understand you perfectly," Mick said. "You want my head on a platter and the rest of my body dismembered. Now let me talk to your wife and I'll leave you in peace." He waited again while the phone was passed to Tamara, grinning when he heard Marshall apologize to his bride for not being an only child.

"So nice to hear from you." Tamara's voice

was sleepy and tinged with amusement. "We've both missed you terribly."

"It's nice to be loved," Mick said. "Listen, I really am sorry to call you, but your hubby swept you away last night before I could talk to you."

"What can I say?" Tamara yawned into the phone. "Love makes a man do desperate things."

"What a coincidence. I'm a little desperate myself. I talked to a woman last night at the reception, a friend of yours. Her name was Stevie or Stephanie, something like that. Petite, black hair, blue eyes... killer smile. What can you tell me about her?"

"Oh... Stevie Knight," Tamara said. "Also known as Stephanie Elizabeth Knight. I went to Vassar with her."

"And?"

"She lives here in San Diego, down by the harbor."

"And?"

"I think the world of her. She's bright, funny, spontaneous..."

"I know *that*."

"She isn't married or engaged, if that's what you mean." Another yawn. "Call her, Mick. I think the two of you would hit it off beautifully. She's in the book. Now can I hang up?"

"Not yet." Mick stood up, cradling the phone between his chin and shoulder while he pulled on a pair of jeans. "It's Friday, so I doubt she'll be home. Do you know where she works?"

"My, my." Tamara's voice sounded clearer

now, as if she'd sat up. "We are impatient, aren't we? She owns a business with a friend of hers, a guy named Morgan Jones. It's called Amazing Events Unlimited, also in the book."

"Just what kind of business has a name like—"

"End of conversation." It was Marshall, and he was clearly running out of patience. "My wife and I have a plane to catch. We're going to spend four lovely weeks cruising the Greek Islands, where strange people like you will not be able to call us at eight o'clock in the morning. Bye-bye, Michael James."

"Hold it! Ask Tamara if Stevie and this Morgan guy are—"

"Sorry, bud. My wife is otherwise occupied. You'll have to find some other woman to annoy."

"I'm trying," Mick said. "I'm trying."

Amazing Events Unlimited occupied a modest office in downtown San Diego, sharing the third floor of the Walker Bank Building with two insurance companies and a collection agency. On rainy days, Stevie practiced diligence, brown bagging her lunch and eating at her desk while she worked. On sunny days she spread a blanket on the narrow strip of grass in front of the building and treated herself to a people-watching picnic. Fortunately, San Diego's mild weather leaned heavily in favor of picnics.

Friday was no exception. The air was sweet, the sky was a beautiful shade of blue, and diligence was out of the question. Stevie curled up on her blanket in the sunshine, sipping an ice-cold soda and watching the world whiz by. She usually enjoyed observing San Diego's noontime feeding frenzy. Today she felt a bit restless, but she wouldn't admit the reason for it. Nor would she acknowledge the hard lifting sensation she felt in her stomach when she uncontrollably conjured up a vision of dark liquid eyes and a wicked male smile.

And so she passed her lunch hour playing leap frog with her thoughts, avoiding the man who lurked at the edge of her consciousness. No, no . . . she would not think about Mick Connover at all: not about his lean, fluid body, not about the hint of humor that shaped his mouth, not about his beguiling, not-so-innocent brown eyes.

Stevie knew herself well, her strengths and her weaknesses. She was a romantic, but she was also a realist. She had learned certain lessons in her childhood that she had no desire to repeat as an adult. Now and forever, she would shy away from men with money and men with power. And Mick Connover possessed a surfeit of both. *Resolution*: She would not dwell on what could not be. End of story. Just like that.

Her resolve was sorely tested when the man she was so determined not to think about suddenly sat down on her blanket. Mick had undergone a metamorphosis since she had last seen him. The expensive tuxedo had been replaced by jeans so old and worn they appeared almost white. His soft denim shirt was sadly in need of ironing, and his dark eyes were hidden by designer sunglasses. Stevie was amazed that she recognized him so quickly.

"Hi, there." He looped his arms around his knees, drawing them up to his chest. "Remember me?"

Stevie could see herself reflected in his sunglasses. Her mouth was hanging open. "Should I?" she asked in a strangled voice.

Mick frowned. "I was afraid of this. You're going to pretend you don't know me again. Considering the fact that I have 'the most incredibly sexy mouth' you have ever seen, you'd think you could remember—"

"All right already. I remember you." He had taken her by surprise; her thoughts were snarled and her senses were prickling. What a way to break a fine resolution. "What are you doing here?"

"You're here," Mick said, as if that explained everything. He let the sight of her spill over him like the warmth of summer sun. She was wearing a yellow knit clingy thing with a wide white belt and strappy woven sandals. Mick was no expert on women's clothes, but this . . . this outfit was pure inspiration. The soft material enhanced her hips and her thighs and the rounded swell of her breasts. The brilliant color contrasted vividly with her glossy black hair and olive complexion. She was bright and beautiful sitting there in the sunshine, and Mick suddenly felt his heart being overwhelmed, his chest expanding uncomfortably. He'd never known a woman who possessed such effortless, natural charm. He felt a little dazed.

"How did you know I was here?" Stevie persisted. She felt lightheaded, warm. Instant sunstroke.

"Tamara," Mick said absently, fascinated by the increasing flush in her cheeks. How interesting. "At the reception you mentioned she was a friend of yours, so I called her this morning."

"This morning?" Stevie's eyes shone in the sunlight, startled. "Good heavens, they were just married—"

"Last night," Mick said, nodding his head. A smile played on that erotic mouth. "You know, I am feeling a little guilty about disturbing them so early. I should have waited until nine or ten to call."

Stevie didn't like his sunglasses. Mick Connover was one of those people who smiled more with his eyes than his lips. She wanted to see his eyes. *I'm going to do something foolish*, she thought. *Again.*

Very gently she took off his sunglasses, laying them on the blanket. His eyes widened briefly in surprise, then transformed into a sunburst of smile lines. It struck Stevie that he had the most expressive eyes of anyone she had ever met. They spoke eloquently, touchingly. Their gazes met in a silent moment of understanding, transcending the currents of disquieting emotion.

"That's better," Stevie said softly, feeling more

at ease, yet more aware. "I like to see someone's eyes when I talk to him."

"You didn't feel that way when you kidnapped me," Mick commented, plucking a blade of grass and chewing on it thoughtfully. "But I suppose that was a special situation. You can't afford to become too friendly with your hostages. All your careful plans could go up in smoke, and then where would you be?"

Stevie squinted into the sunlight. Quietly, "You're so right."

He'd touched a nerve, though he wasn't sure how. He watched her for a moment, noticing the way her lashes made teardrop shadows against her cheeks. Some sort of wariness and vague regret briefly robbed her face of all animation. Mick was surprised, and momentarily disturbed. A protective, almost painful stab of tenderness made him say quickly, "I don't want to seem vulgarly inquisitive—gently bred fellow that I am—but my imagination is running amok. Do you really specialize in amazing events unlimited?"

Stevie laughed then, blue eyes flicking sideways to his. "Morgan came up with the name," she said. "We started the business three years ago, after one of our friends asked us to help with a surprise party for his wife's birthday. She was a real estate agent, so Morgan and I posed as newlyweds looking for a house. When we went to her office we were madly in love, holding hands and drooling over each other. He was my 'sugar lips.' I was his 'sweet cakes.' We were so convincing, it was almost sickening."

"I can imagine," Mick said, and he could. He found the thought of Morgan and Stevie nuzzling each other a little sickening, himself.

"She drove us to Sunnyside to look at a little ranch house, and that was the beginning of the end. Our marriage disintegrated right before her eyes. Every house we looked at inspired a new battle. After two hours, I was hysterical. I jumped out of the car and ran into a restaurant and locked myself in the ladies' room. Morgan convinced the poor woman to follow me and try to talk me out. Of course, her friends were waiting in the restaurant to surprise her... and the rest is history."

"I see. And you and Morgan..." Mick hesitated, wondering how to tactfully phrase his question. *Do you still drool over each other?*

"We're partners," Stevie said, misunderstanding. "It's incredible how much the business has grown. For the most part, Morgan and I keep busy on the administrative end now. We hire students from the drama department at the university to work for us during the winter. In the summer, when the kids are out of school, we fill in. Morgan's an actor, so he loves it."

Mick smiled, making an effort to disguise the emotions she'd dredged up in him. "I don't think he's the only one. You seemed to enjoy yourself the other night."

Stevie sighed. She could pretend she didn't

know what he was talking about, but somehow she didn't think that would work with Mick Connover. "I suppose you're never going to let me forget that, are you?"

Mick smiled; it was an angelic smile. "Forget what, Stevie-Stephanie?"

Her eyes met his squarely. "You are no gentleman, M. J. Connover."

"You're right." Still smiling, he lifted her chin on the arc of his finger and leaned closer. "I'm no gentleman. Consider yourself warned, sweet cakes."

Stevie's gaze wandered over his face, touching briefly and inevitably on his mouth. *Oh, that mouth...* "I'm late," she said suddenly, pulling away from him. "I should get back to work."

Mick shrugged and got to his feet, helping her fold the blanket. "Why the rush? Does Morgan dock your pay if you take a long lunch hour?"

"Morgan has nothing to do with it." Stevie picked up the empty soda can, shoving it into her crumpled lunch sack. "As a matter of fact, he's in Los Angeles today filming a commercial. I simply have a great deal of work to take care of." She paused to take a breath, then hoisted the blanket under one arm and stuck out her hand. "It's been very nice running into you again, Mr. Connover."

"Don't you do that well, though?" Mick whistled in mock admiration. "Such a polite little speech, right down to the 'Mr.' Connover. I'm impressed. If I were a gentleman, I'd certainly take the hint. Unfortunately..."

She threw him a look that said, *I should have known*. ". . . you're no gentleman."

"Sad but true." He took her hand, bringing it slowly to his lips. The kiss he placed on her palm was no more than a whisper. "Who knows? Maybe you'll be a good influence on me."

Stevie pulled her hand away, but the movement was gentle, almost absentminded. She wasn't going to be any sort of influence on Mick Connover. Sad but true. She looked up into his eyes, trying on a smile for size. It didn't fit. "Well, it's been lovely—"

"Hell, don't start that again." Mick dismissed her second polite little speech with a wave of his hand. A small corner of his spirit felt a little bruised, but he wasn't the type to let it show. Surely she felt it, that sense of intensity between them. Didn't she?

He turned, looking at the office building behind them with a great show of interest. "Your office is here?"

"Yes." Her tone was wary.

"I'd like to see it." He smiled at her, playing the innocent, all the while wanting to touch her in the worst way. "Have you got a few minutes to show me around?"

"You'd be disappointed," Stevie said. She was quite familiar with the Connover Building, the crown of San Diego's skyline. "It isn't what you're used to, believe me."

There was a short pause. "What am I used to, if you don't mind my asking?"

"There are restrooms in the Connover Building larger than our entire office."

He eyed her with solemn humor. "And you're assuming I spend a great deal of time in the restrooms of the Connover Building?"

"Never mind." She'd said too much already. The wind was picking up a bit, pulling her hair across her mouth and eyes. She brushed it back with her hand, squinting west, toward the ocean. Clouds were piling up on the horizon, a dark warning between the water and sky. When had that happened? "You brought a rainstorm with you, M. J. Connover. There wasn't a cloud in the sky until you came along."

He grinned, holding her in a lazy gaze. "What can I say? I'm a disruptive personality."

"Yes, you are," Stevie said with great conviction.

He slipped his hands into his pockets and tilted his head thoughtfully. He was trying to decide how eyes that viewed him with such caution could look so warm and enticing at the same time. "I'll make you a deal, Stevie-Stephanie. Take me inside and show me your office and I'll forgive you."

"Forgive me?" She smiled curiously. "Forgive me for what?"

"You're standing on my sunglasses, sweet cakes."

*   *   *

It seemed to be a "regulation" office. Velvety charcoal-gray carpet, generic leather couch and matching end tables. Nice music, nice watercolor prints on the wall, nice magazines on the end tables. A fresh-faced receptionist smiled behind a half-moon desk. Any dentist would have felt right at home.

"The outer sanctum," Stevie said, gesturing like a game show host. "As you can see, it's all very businesslike and not at all interesting."

Mick knew better. To the right of the reception desk was a door with a plaque reading *Thespian*. "Morgan's office," he guessed. Then, when Stevie nodded, he pointed to the innocent-looking door on the right. "And what's behind door number two?"

"Mostly . . . chaos." Stevie smiled and opened the door to her office, stepping back to let him enter. "Enter at your own risk, M. J. Connover."

Mick was fascinated by Stevie's office. Here was a treasure chest of answers. The carpet, the draperies, and the soft leather chair were all creamy white. There was a pair of battered white sneakers in the corner. The window sill held several anemic-looking potted plants. There was an empty bag of M & M's in the garbage can and a full bag on her desk. Her "in" basket was full and her "out" basket was empty.

Ergo, he drew his conclusions. Her favorite color was white. She walked to work. She did not have a green thumb. She was a chocolate addict.

She preferred sunshine and picnics to paperwork. Clearly a woman with her priorities in order.

He picked up a photograph on her desk, feeling his teeth grind together as he studied it. It wasn't a pleasant picture. Stevie tucked beneath Morgan's arm in a blaze of sunshine, fitting perfectly. They looked completely...comfortable ...with each other. Mick had friends and family, he had close relationships with intelligent and caring female companions, but he couldn't think of a single person in the world he was truly comfortable with. He envied them that.

He envied Morgan.

"When was this taken?" he asked, trying to sound casual.

"Last September. Morgan's sister was visiting, and we took her to Disneyland." Stevie smiled, remembering Morgan's reluctance to leave the park at closing time. "Morgan's one of the original Lost Boys, content never to grow up. In the past three years, he has dragged me to Disneyland at least twenty times. Which says something for our relationship, since I'm afraid of heights and have a very fragile stomach."

"You've been together three years?" *Come on, Stevie. Tell me what I want to know without making me blurt it out. My pride is at stake here. And possibly my heart.*

"Almost. We opened the business three years ago in September."

Mick sighed heavily and replaced the photograph on her desk. So carefully, though his instinct was to simply drop the thing. "Isn't that nice," he said.

Stevie smiled uncertainly. Her social conversation had just about been used up, and Mick didn't look as if he had anything more to say. It was an awkward moment. Ordinarily Stevie was an expert at putting people at ease, at making strangers feel like friends. With this man, her strongest impulse was to fight the feelings he invoked in her. If it had begun as a game, it had ceased to be one rather abruptly. Nervously she tapped the toe of one shoe, throwing a quick glance around the office. "Well, you've had the grand tour."

He met her eyes and smiled faintly. "Why are you so afraid of me?"

She stared at him. She couldn't have looked away if her life had depended on it. "You're a dangerous man, M. J. Connover," she said finally.

His smile stretched. Apparently he wasn't the only one capable of a direct hit. "I'm a pussycat, Stevie-Stephanie. Will you please go out with me tonight?"

"No," she said softly. She didn't stop to think about it. She *couldn't* stop to think about it.

"Why?" His eyes revealed nothing beyond polite curiosity.

"It would be too ... complicated."

"Really?" His head tilted slightly. Though he still smiled, his throat was dry and tight. "And here I thought I was such a simple man. What you see is what you get, and all that. Do you know something I don't?"

"I know myself," Stevie said softly. Try as she might, she couldn't deny the power of his physical presence. He overwhelmed her in every possible way: the sweet suggestion in his smile, the shadow of doubt in his expressive brown eyes, the softly faded denim caressing his legs. She moved around the desk, sliding the chair in, glancing at the scattered papers there in a distracted, restless fashion. She couldn't imagine what to say or do next.

Mick took a deep breath. "Are you and Morgan—?"

"What?" Stevie's eyes widened with sudden understanding. *"Morgan?* Believe me, getting romantically involved with Morgan has never even entered my mind."

It may have never entered your mind, Mick thought, but I'll bet your old pal Morgan has thought of it once or twice. "Why? Is he complicated, too?"

Uncomfortable, she turned to the window. "Never mind. You wouldn't understand."

"Irrational behavior confuses me," Mick admitted.

"If you think I'm irrational, I'm surprised you're still here." *Childish, Stevie. That was very childish.*

He came up beside her, looking out the window at nothing. His shoulder brushed hers, and he heard her indrawn breath. The air was filled with feelings, demanding and unfamiliar. Questions without answers. After a short pause, he said, "Stevie?"

She turned her head a little, the expression in her eyes something between panic and anticipation. "What?"

She was so close, he could practically feel the heat from her little upturned nose. He inhaled her scent with every breath, and thoughts he didn't dare speak came and went in his mind. His voice was as calm and controlled as he could possibly make it. "I probably should warn you. I don't deal with rejection very well."

And I don't deal with temptation very well, Stevie thought, her eyes focusing on the curve of his smile. Trying to clear her distracting thoughts, she said huskily, "You're a Connover. You probably haven't had much practice."

There it was again, that certain tone in her voice. He touched her cheek with the back of his hand, his eyes revealing his curiosity. "And here I've come to the pageant without my swimming suit."

That got her attention. "What did you say?"

He shrugged and stepped back, turning his attention again to the window. A dirty gray thunderhead was spreading across the sky, turning day to night. "I'm getting the distinct impression I'm being judged here. You should have told me. I would have taken time to iron my shirt. Is there a talent competition? I can play a killer version of 'Hey Jude' on the French horn."

There was a new tension now, one she couldn't quite understand. "I'm not judging you." Her voice was thick and strange and unconvincing.

"No? I could have sworn you were." He glanced back at her, his gaze whimsical, yet curiously guarded. "Just what do I have to do to make a good impression on you, Stevie-Stephanie? Ride my bike past your house with no hands? Carry your books to school? Stand on my head and recite the Pledge of Allegiance?"

Stevie laughed in spite of herself. "That's pretty serious stuff."

He nodded. "It worked on Ramona Bagley in third grade."

I'll bet it did, Stevie thought, gazing at the boyish smile that lingered about his mouth. The air around them filled with a thick silence. His expression held a trace of humor, but she saw something else there, something feverish and hungry. He dipped his head and rubbed his cheek softly against hers. A gentle motion, yet the heat between them was powerful. She put her hands flat on his chest, feeling the warmth there. Her fingers trembled.

The telephone shattered the unearthly silence. Stevie's arms dropped to her sides; turning around, she groped for the receiver and picked up her stapler. Cheeks burning, she tried again. "Hello?"

"I was wonderful." It was Morgan.

"Were you?" There was an unmistakable

tremor in her voice. Mick's eyes were boring into her back.

"I was indeed," Morgan said. "You should have seen me. I had the most realistic sinus head-ache in the history of television commercials. So how are things at the office? Are you surviving without me?"

"Just barely," she replied hoarsely. Mick had come up behind her, burying his face in her hair. She felt his lips against the side of her neck, and the temperature of her body rose like the tide. She closed her eyes and tried to concentrate. "So when do you think you'll be back, Morgan?"

"I probably won't make it back to the office today. You know how the freeways are between L.A. and San Diego." A short pause here. "Are you all right? You sound . . . strange."

"I feel strange," Stevie said, but she wasn't talking to Morgan. Her respiration was shallow, unsatisfying. Mick's hand cupped her cheek, drawing her face toward him. She could see the shimmering darkness of his eyes, with their star-tling, gold-flecked irises. Such beautiful eyes, and so easy to get lost in . . .

"Strange?" Morgan barked. It was the second time he had repeated the word. "What do you mean, strange? Are you sick?"

"Not sick," Stevie said on a whisper of breath. Still holding the phone, her arm dropped limply to her side. Mick's eyes blurred as he came closer, filling her vision. He seemed to hesitate for a moment, then his lips closed over hers, dragging back and forth with an urgent, questing pressure that left her stinging and dazed. He had stopped catering to her defenses. He couldn't have made it plainer. The kiss was purposeful and devastating, a blinding glimpse of sensual pleasure.

He broke from her abruptly, staring into her eyes. Whatever he read there seemed to satisfy him. A shaky smile passed over his mouth, infinitely tender. He touched the hot curve of her cheek with a soothing finger, then turned and walked out of the room.

Stevie stood quite still for the longest time, a prisoner of arms that no longer held her. Eventually a muted expletive invaded her trance, drawing her eyes to the telephone receiver in her hand.

Oh, dear. Morgan.

She lifted the receiver to her ear, wincing as she heard Morgan call down a curse on Ma Bell's head. The man had a short fuse and a creative vocabulary, a nasty combination. "I'm sorry," she said, interrupting his tirade. "I dropped the phone."

"Dropped the phone? Where the hell did you drop it, out the damn window?"

"I need to go now."

"Wait a minute—"

"Drive carefully," she said huskily. She touched unsteady fingertips to her swollen lips. "I think there's a hurricane coming."

Chapter

4

STEVIE HAD A SNEAKING suspicion that Morgan would come calling that night. She wasn't disappointed. His car skidded to a halt in front of her apartment building just as the rumbling sky split open in a deluge that peppered her carpet through an open window. Morgan never simply *parked* his car. That was too tame for him. He had to make a great deal of noise, and leave a signature of burning rubber.

She hurried to close the window, noticing the set of Morgan's shoulders as he ran from the car to the building. Those were not the shoulders of a happy man.

She put a towel down over the drenched carpet, then went to the front door and opened it. Morgan was there, his fist raised to knock. Or, judging by the expression on his face, to pound.

"No one hangs up on me," he said.

She sighed. "Hi, Morgan."

"It drives me crazy when people hang up on me, you know that." He walked past her, shaking the raindrops out of his wild blond hair. "So are you mad or sick or what?"

"Come in, won't you?" she added quite unnecessarily, wiping a stray drop from her cheek.

"So what's the deal?" He sat down on her couch and put his feet up on her coffee table. Clearly he wasn't going to budge until he had an explanation.

Stevie pushed his feet off the table none too gently. "There is no great crisis, Morgan. I was busy when you called. It's as simple as that."

"Ha!" He threw back his head in a well-practiced theatrical gesture. "I know you better than that, buddy. I know when there's . . ." His voice trailed off as he took a good hard look at Stevie. "Good heavens, woman. Good heavens . . . what happened to you? Why do you look like that?"

Stevie knew precisely what she looked like. Her hair was steaming in hot oil beneath a ruffled plastic cap. Aloe vera eye cream greased the delicate area around her eyes; avocado night cream lent her cheeks a translucent green shimmer. Her favorite stormy-night robe was coming apart at the seams and missing four buttons. At the moment she had it belted with a fluorescent pink scarf, an interesting contrast to the red and green argyle socks she wore.

She feigned surprise with a dramatically lifted brow. "I don't know what you're talking about."

Morgan's eyes dragged over her slowly, head to toe. "Egad . . . the hair. That puffy robe thing. Your skin, what happened to your beautiful skin?"

Stevie curled up on a chintz settee opposite him. "Good skin isn't an accident. It takes work."

"It *looks* like an accident," Morgan said, mesmerized by her new color. "I've never seen this side of you before, dear. So . . . frightening."

She smiled sweetly. "I'm glad I hung up on you."

He settled back against the cushions, crossing his arms over his chest. "Well, if you think you're going to scare me away with your Halloween costume, you have another think coming. I want to know why you hung up on me."

"I told you. I was busy."

Silence. Morgan was thinking, his eyes shaded by heavy gold lashes. Then, softly, "You had a visitor."

"Did I?" Stevie avoided his gaze, hitching up her socks.

"You did." His smile told her he knew he was on the right track. "M. J. Connover, if I don't miss my guess . . . and I never do. The self-same individual you so wantonly attacked just the other night—"

"You're not on the stage, Morgan." Stevie cuddled more deeply into the chair. "Try to curb the theatrics."

"So tell me," he said simply.

Morgan was a good friend. He was practical in

his own extravagant way, generous and empathetic. He was also a sensualist, a connoisseur of women, adoring one and all with a loving impartiality. No one was *particularly* necessary to him, yet all were beloved.

Stevie had been an exception. On the first day they met, he had looked her over like a stray kitten he was contemplating adopting. For whatever reason, he had cast himself in the role of protector, then friend. Over the years Stevie had grown to love him in a purely platonic way. He was the brother she never had. She looked up to him. More importantly, she trusted him.

"You're right," she said softly, looking at her hands in her lap. "Mick was in the office when you called. I didn't mean to hang up on you, but I was . . . rattled."

"Ho! That'll be the day. Stevie Knight rattled by a mere man?"

"He isn't a 'mere' man," she said gloomily. She raised her eyes and looked into his, and found they were gentle, whimsical. "I'm on the edge of something, Morgan. And it's scaring me."

"Green face cream is scary," Morgan said. "Those socks of yours are scary. Having a relationship with someone you're attracted to is *not* scary."

"Oh, but it is. You know his background. Ancient money. Navy blue blood."

With great earnestness, Morgan said, "Angel, you're confused. Having money is good. Not having money is bad. Do you see how simple that is?"

Stevie's smile curved into melancholy lines. "It's not always that simple, Morgan."

"Of course it is, just that simple. If a little money is nice, a great deal of money is even nicer. Women just enjoy complicating things. They don't like a straight and narrow road. They like twisted, bumpy, convoluted, mind-boggling—"

"You're getting dramatic again, Morgan."

"Excuse me." He frowned. "Now where was I? Oh, yes. Don't worry about the man's background, love. Worry about the man. Worry about whether he chews with his mouth open or drools when he sleeps. Important things. Who knows? He might turn out to be a terrific guy. Of course, you might also discover he's a jerk, in which case I will personally separate his shoulders from his head. Either way, a happy ending. Now, have we cleared everything up here?"

"I feel so much better," Stevie said, putting an overdose of sincerity in her voice. "Thank you for dropping by."

"No problem at all." Morgan stood up, raking his hand through rain-damp hair. "I'm glad I could help. I must say, it's refreshing to see you breaking your Milquetoast habit."

"My what?"

"The men you date, Stevie. Milquetoast. Long on sincerity, short on personality. Take that baby-faced shoe salesman you went out with last week—"

Stevie straightened her spine and lifted her

chin. "Evan Oman is one of the most dependable men—"

"I rest my point. Dependable is very nice if you're looking for a pet doggie. A serious relationship calls for a flesh and blood human being, and I'm not at all sure Evan qualifies. Don't snarl at me, I'm through preaching. I would like you to answer a question for me, though." He smiled encouragingly. "Please?"

Morgan never said please. Stevie stared at him suspiciously. "That depends on the question."

His eyes were bright, like sunshine through a green forest. "Do you go to bed with all this grease on you every night?"

Stevie got to her feet, patting the ruffled plastic cap self-consciously. "Well . . . yes. Lately I have."

He whistled softly, running his finger down the super-slick curve of her nose. "How do you sleep? Don't you slip off the bed?"

"I have a birthday coming up, all right? I'm going to be . . ." She took a deep breath and closed her eyes. "Thirty."

"What the hell does a birthday have to do with—"

"Never mind! You're a man, Morgan. You wouldn't understand."

Like all fine actors, Morgan had an innate sense of timing. Whatever he saw in Stevie's eyes convinced him it was time to leave. "I will leave you to marinate in peace," he said cheerfully, bolting for the door. "Have a lovely weekend. I'll call you later."

Long after Morgan had gone, Stevie wandered restlessly through the apartment. Ordinarily her home gave her great pleasure. She had furnished it with whimsy and love and a beguiling sense of individual style. The colors melted together with a Victorian elegance. The walls were covered with a glistening violet and cream silk. Soft white lacework draped the semicircular windows. There were Victorian lamps, antique dolls, patchwork pillows, and pale watercolors. Beautiful things. Her things.

But tonight . . . tonight she was distracted, unable to settle. She was oblivious to the comfort of the pretty rooms. Finally, without consciously making the decision, she went to the top shelf in her bedroom closet and brought forth a dusty white photo album. Her fingers slowly traced the embossed gold lettering on the front: *Memories*.

She took the album to her bed, studying each and every photograph with intense concentration. Baby Stephanie in a carriage in front of a white Georgian mansion. Stephanie riding her first pony, Stephanie at camp, at boarding school. Stephanie skiing in Switzerland. Stephanie at a garden party on the White House lawn.

There were several pictures of nannies and tutors and schoolmates, few photographs of her parents. It seemed they were always absent when the camera was brought out.

She dropped the album on the floor and snug-

gled deep into her bed. There were so many
things in her mind. The years she spent in that
sterile white mansion. The polished marble floors
that had always felt so cold to bare feet. The intense, humorless eyes of her father; the pale
blue, vaguely preoccupied gaze of her mother.
Home sweet home.

It had been ten years since the princess had
left her ivory tower to become a working stiff.
She'd become Stevie. She'd learned happiness, a
bit late, but she turned out to be quite good at it.
And if she bore any resentment at all, she direct-
ed it toward the almighty dollar. She'd been in
competition with it for so many years, always
coming in a poor second. When and if she fell in
love, she promised herself, she would come first.

Stevie turned over on her side and pressed her
hand against the burning knot in her middle. Her
fragile stomach, an early warning system for
trouble on its way.

She thought of Mick. Briefly, hesitantly, like a
guilty secret. His deep brown eyes had a tenderness that a saint would have envied. She could
almost believe . . .

But she didn't allow herself to finish the
thought. She closed her eyes, tight, willing sleep
to come. Tomorrow would be soon enough to
make a foolish mistake.

In honor of her upcoming birthday, Stevie had
adopted an exercise regime. Nothing too strenu-
ous—a few isometric exercises at her desk on the

weekdays and a short run on the weekends. Extremely short.

Saturday morning dawned bright and beautiful. A warming sun was baking the moisture from the earth in misty little spirals. Stevie dressed in her new jogging suit and tied a pretty yellow scarf around her forehead. She liked to look as though she knew what she was doing, though she had never gone farther than four blocks before her lungs collapsed and her knees buckled. Still, she persevered. Today she had high hopes of making it to the local convenience store and back, a five block marathon.

She stretched out in front of her apartment building, propping her leg high on the weathered brick and trying not to groan with pain. She promised to reward herself with a chocolate donut. Thank heavens she wasn't overweight. Her body operated entirely on an incentive system.

She did quite well for the first thirty seconds. A nice pace, no pressure, no gasping for air. Until the beat-up black Jeep pulled up beside her, inching along at a steady three miles an hour. Mick Connover saluted her from the driver's seat.

"Beautiful morning for running," he said cheerfully. The Jeep was open; his hair was tousled and his skin was fresh and wind-reddened.

"What are you doing here?" Stevie kept her words to a minimum; she needed the oxygen.

"I need to talk to you." He braked for a fearless

kitty, then caught up with her again. "I pulled up in front of your apartment building just as you turned the corner. Are you happy to see me?"

"I'm surprised to see you." He looked terribly good to her in the hazy morning light, his face softened into youthful contours, his eyes drowsy with the residue of sleep. He was wearing a white T-shirt under a stone-washed Levi jacket, the cuffs rolled loosely above the wrists. He was far more appealing than a chocolate donut, and had he been waiting for her at the store, she would have made it there in record time.

Unfortunately, he wasn't waiting there. He was rolling along beside her at a snail's pace. Already her lungs were beginning to burn and her knees were up to mischief. If she attempted to run for any respectable length of time, she would collapse and die on the streets of San Diego. If she followed her planned route—all five blocks —Mick Connover would see her as the pathetic physical specimen she really was. She really wasn't sure which was worse.

"I try to run six miles every morning," Mick said. "Helps wake me up."

Six miles? Stevie nearly tripped over a fire hydrant. "You needed to talk to me?" she asked, her voice fraying around the edges.

"Yes, I did." Mick's voice was dreamy. He was appreciating Stevie's form. "I have someone I want you to meet."

"Who?" She was beginning to feel light-headed.

Mischief sparkled in the depths of his eyes. "It's a surprise. How many miles do you usually jog?"

Ha. "Oh, it varies." Then, on sudden inspiration: "Why don't you get a cup of coffee or something and I'll meet you back at my apartment when I'm through?" She could always go sit in the park for an hour.

"I have a better idea." His lips curved into a slow smile. "I'll park up ahead and run with you. We can jog down to the harbor and around the park and back."

Stevie staggered to a halt, doubled over at the waist, and stared at the cracks in the sidewalk. "That's at least five miles," she gasped.

"Actually it's not quite three," Mick said thoughtfully. "That's not much of a workout. If you'd like, we could double the course."

She raised her head and glowered at him. "Why don't we just run to Los Angeles while we're at it?"

Again that blistering, damnably innocent smile. "Why don't you just get in the car, sweet cakes? Fun is fun, but you're just a beginner. You shouldn't push it."

He didn't have to ask twice. Pride was a poor substitute for oxygen. Stevie climbed into the Jeep and collapsed on the soft leather seat. When she could catch her breath—which wasn't soon —she asked weakly, "How did you know I'd just started jogging?"

"You mean, besides the fact you nearly passed

out after four minutes?" His eyes had become very bright. "Your running shoes are so new they practically squeak."

"They're killing me," Stevie muttered. She squinted through the front windshield as he pulled into traffic. "Where are we going?"

"I told you. There's someone I want you to meet."

Stevie's yellow headband had drooped endearingly over one eyebrow. She pushed it up, blue eyes startled beneath windy bangs. "I can't meet anyone dressed like this."

"Fine." Mick was feeling generous. It was a beautiful day, and his beautiful lady was exhibiting less of a fighting spirit. He was encouraged. "I'll take you home to change. You don't have any kidnappings or anything planned for today, do you?"

"Not a one," Stevie said wistfully. "It kind of takes the spark out of the weekend."

"Poor thing." He reached out a hand, rubbing his index finger gently beneath her chin. "I'll have to see what I can do about putting it back in."

Her apartment was exactly what he had expected. Tasteful, eye-catching, mysterious, and romantic... a perfect home for the kissing bandit. While she changed he wandered round the living room, trying to absorb the essence of her from the things around him. He touched the fringe on the Victorian lamps, played the antique music boxes, glanced through the rows of books

in the maple hutch. She had an incredible variety
of reading material, from classics to comic books
to romances. He pulled out a copy of *The
Masons and Builders Bible* and laughed out loud.
Only Stevie.

Stevie walked in, tugging a brush through her
hair. "What's so amusing?"

"You." He replaced the book, still smiling.
"You are truly the most unpredictable woman I
have ever met. The last time I saw a room like
this, it was in a museum, roped off with a red
velvet cord. It's perfect."

Stevie found her gaze drawn irresistibly to the
long stretch of his legs in the well-worn denim.
There was a primitive appeal in the way the soft
fabric molded his muscles, and she studied that
masculine form with faithful attention, until she
realized just what it was she was doing. *Good
grief, Stephanie . . . you're turning into a lech in
your old age.* "Perfect for what?" she asked
quickly, brushing her hair with renewed vigor.

"Answers," Mick said softly. He had felt her
eyes on him, felt the part of her that was reaching
out, wanting to let down her guard, but not quite
prepared for the consequences. She looked
heartbreakingly beautiful, with her brave blue
eyes and the siren's curves of her woman's body.
He'd known women who had worn their sexual-
ity blatantly, leaving nothing to the heart or
mind. Stevie was a changeling, at times holding
back, at times weighing, occasionally giving free
reign to her innate sensuality. He was reluctant to

take his eyes off her. He had to understand her. He needed to be able to anticipate her. Still, he wondered if even that would be enough for him, if he would ever be able to get close enough.

Stevie had watched the emotions flickering in his eyes, trying to read him. Suddenly it occurred to her that the silence had stretched to an awkward length. "What kind of answers are you looking for?" she asked, trying to pick up the thread of the conversation.

"That's for you to know and me to find out."

Her breath caught in her throat as she absorbed the picture he made, standing there studying her as if it was the most important thing he had ever done. His lips were curved with the erotic smile that had fascinated and excited her from the beginning. She dropped the hairbrush.

Time to talk again, Stevie. You keep drifting away. "So, tell me." She smoothed the silky white skirt she wore, touched the clingy white top. "Do I look all right to meet your friend?"

"My friend is going to be very impressed," Mick said softly. He walked across the room and took her hand in his. "May I have the pleasure of this day, Stevie-Stephanie?"

Her gaze found their joined hands and lingered there before returning to his face. She sighed once, in honor of all her good intentions, then smiled. She would allow herself this much, then. One summer's day. There was an idyll trembling in the air, and she couldn't resist it.

Still, she didn't want to give in too easily. "As

a rule," she said, "the kidnapper does not social-
ize with the kidnapee."

Low lights kindled in his eyes. "I like breaking
rules."

"You're pretty self-confident for a kidnapee."

"I'm a Connover," he said. "It's a trademark."

Hand in hand, the kidnapee led a willing kidnapper to the car. For some reason, Stevie had
expected him to drive into the heart of the city.
Instead he turned toward Escondido. The noise
level on the freeway made conversation impossible. Stevie ducked her head to escape the thrash-
ing wind, tucking her skirt firmly between her
legs to keep it in place. This wasn't at all the sort
of car she expected a self-confident Connover to
own. A Ferrari would have been more in keeping
with her prejudices. Instead he arrived in an
open-top Jeep that was probably very nice for
climbing mountains, but a little drafty on the
freeway. Her hair would never be the same, but
she didn't really mind. She felt her defenses falling away like so much sand.

He left the freeway at Escondido, heading the
Jeep up a scrubby little mountain patchworked
with avocado farms and a few small ranches. It
wasn't an exclusive area, by any means. There
were more horses and chickens than swimming
pools, and the narrow road could have used a
good resurfacing.

"Your friend lives here?" Stevie asked curiously.

"Uh-huh. Has done for several years."

"Is he a farmer?"

Mick gave her a sudden, amused look. "He tries to be. He's not very successful, but he's determined."

"Oh." She paused thoughtfully. "What does he raise?"

"Horses, cattle, chickens, tomatoes, avocados, oranges, lemons, grapefruit, cantaloupe, lettuce, beans, and squash."

"Good grief." Her skirt caught the wind and billowed playfully around her seat before she captured it again. "He must have an enormous place."

"Not really." He turned the Jeep into a fenced drive lined with young avocado trees. "See for yourself, Stevie-Stephanie. This is it."

It did not take a particular gift for perception to realize that Mick was nursing an amusing secret. Stevie stared at the small stucco house with two picture windows overlooking a thirsty patch of flowers. The lawn looked as if it had just been mowed, but needed to be watered. There were no cars in the gravel driveway, only a rugged set of tire tracks that might have been left by a four-wheel-drive Jeep.

"It's yours," she said incredulously. "*You* live here, don't you?"

He bumped over a fat green garden hose and killed the engine. Then he turned to look at her, his arm stretched across the back of her seat. "My mother calls it the 'little adobe thing.' I've lived here for nearly four years." Then, when

Stevie continued to stare at him in that transfixed way, he added, "Why so quiet? Don't you like it?"

Don't you like it? Stevie smiled faintly at his choice of words, at the boyish anxiety in his voice. "I like it," she said. "I'm just . . . surprised. You told me you wanted me to meet someone."

"I do," he replied equitably. "Me." He lifted his hand, brushing the windblown hair from her face. He gave the task his somber, undivided attention, his eyes narrowed against the harsh white sunlight. At last he said, "It seemed to me you were a little sensitive when it came to my background. I had the feeling I was being sentenced without being given a fair trial. Call me crazy, but I kind of like to give people a chance to know me before they condemn me."

"I wasn't condemning anyone," Stevie said uncomfortably. Without the rumble of the Jeep's engine and the rush of wind in her ears, her voice seemed unusually loud.

"Maybe not." He looked at her, and the gentle amusement was missing from his soft brown eyes. "But you weren't about to give me a fair chance, Stevie-Stephanie. And that's all I want from you—a fair chance. I don't spend my days in the Connover Building, posturing in a three-piece suit. I own a sporting goods store near the marina, and more often than not, I wear shorts to work. Usually I make a profit, occasionally I don't. On weekends I spend my time trying to keep my garden alive, a never-ending battle.

Plants don't like me, but I like them. I have one horse, one cow, and six laying hens. When my parents visit—which isn't often—they come with a can of Lysol. There you have it, the story of my life."

Stevie swallowed hard. "As simple as that?"

He shrugged. "I told you I was a simple guy. You just wouldn't believe me."

"Your family—"

"Disapproves of me completely." His smile was slow. "But they can't *help* but love me. Would you like to see my house?"

The sky was a sweet oiled blue and the breeze kicked at her hair, pulling it away from Stevie's face. The air was sweet with the wind-dusted fragrance of his skin, surrounding her. She felt a warm sensation deep within, a part of her that had been tense for the longest time beginning to relax.

Her smile grew slowly, like his. "I'd love to see your house."

Chapter
5

MICK SEEMED DIFFERENT SOMEHOW, here in this
house he had made a home. Younger, yet more
sure of himself. He showed her around with a
contagious enthusiasm, skimming over the dirty
dishes in the kitchen sink and the ironing piled in
the utility room. He paid particular attention to
the kitchen cabinets he had installed himself, the
oak wainscoting in the dining room, and the new
wallpaper in the living room.

"I put it up myself," he said, touching a seam
that was almost, but not quite, even. "It was the
first time I'd tried it. I wasted an entire roll before I got the hang of it. Couldn't get the paste
out of my hair for days."

Stevie's eyes twinkled with droll understanding. Morgan had insisted on hanging the wall-

paper in her apartment, much to her dismay. After six days and three buckets of paste spilled on her carpet, she had broken into tears and kicked him out. "I gave up and finally hired a wallpaper hanger," she said, instinctively avoiding Morgan's name. Mick didn't seem to like the sound of it, and she wanted nothing to spoil this day. "Of course, it was peanut butter and jelly sandwiches for two weeks after," she added with a sigh. "Wallpaper hangers don't come cheap."

Mick eyed her thoughtfully. "So how do you feel about peanut butter and jelly sandwiches? I don't know about you, but I'm ready for lunch."

"I jogged nearly six blocks this morning—"

"Five."

"—and I didn't even get a chocolate donut for my efforts. I'm starving."

"Great." He shucked off his jacket and tossed it over the back of the sofa. "We'll picnic with Dumbo Williams."

"*Who*?"

The corners of his mouth tilted into a charming, trust-me smile. A gentle finger tapped up her chin. "Dumbo Williams. He lives in the pasture behind the garden. Not to worry, sweet cakes. You're going to love him."

She loved Dumbo Williams.

He was a horse, or so Mick said, though he was the size of a small donkey. He had glorious black eyes and soft fluffy ears that looked two sizes too large for his head. Dumbo ears. He picnicked on clover on one side of the fence; Mick and Stevie had peanut butter and jam sandwiches on the other. Judging by the soulful look in Dumbo's eyes, Stevie thought he would rather have had a sandwich.

"Why Williams?" Stevie asked, stretching out her legs on the quilt Mick had provided. Her feet were bare, her shoes half hidden in the long meadow grass. Stevie was rarely in her shoes for long.

"One of the ranchers up the road gave him to me," Mick replied, tossing Dumbo a crust of bread. "Frank Williams. It seemed logical."

"Do you ride him?" she asked doubtfully.

"Look at those stubby little legs. He'd go flat down on his belly if I even tried." He flopped full-length on the blanket beside her, hooking his arms behind his head. "Dumbo isn't exactly useful, but he provides atmosphere. Kind of like my garden."

"I like your garden," Stevie protested. She thought it was utterly charming, with all those crooked little rows and the seed packets stuck on wooden stakes to identify the anemic-looking vegetables. Here was a side of Mick Connover she never would have imagined in a thousand years—the struggling farmer. "Do you get much produce from it?"

"Last year I got an onion." He grinned. "At least, I think it was an onion. I faced the facts a long time ago. If I was going to have a garden, it would only be because I enjoyed *gardening*, not because I wanted to reap the fruits of my labors. I'm much happier now that my expectations are lowered."

Stevie smiled, sun-warmed and content and at peace with the world. Grass tickled her bare toes at the edge of the quilt. The soft breeze ruffled the dark cloud of her hair around her face. She felt very much at home, secure enough to allow herself a thorough appreciation of the man beside her. His lazy smile was an endearment. His silky-soft hair tumbled over his forehead, showing a tendency to part in the middle. His smooth skin was sun-tinted in fever colors—amber and gold, a warm pink stain beneath his cheekbones. For the longest time she just looked at him, never even blinking when he caught and held her eyes.

"You're staring," he said softly.

"I know." She smiled, noticing the way the sun fell like a halo around his head. "I can't help it. Did you know you were incredibly easy on the eyes, M. J. Connover?"

That startled him. He rose up on one elbow, his body shifting slightly toward her. His gaze was soft and steady, a bit quizzical. "Thank you."

"You're welcome."

"You're very nice yourself."

Her eyes drifted down to his incredibly sexy mouth. "Thank you very much."

He returned to his prone position, one arm shielding his eyes from the sun. *Stevie, if I don't touch you soon . . .*

Stevie used the awkward moment construc-
tively, making a silent list of the places on his face
and body at which she didn't dare to look. She
had had so many reasons for keeping this man at
a distance, and suddenly they counted for nothing. All the hesitation and confusion of the past
few days disappeared in the softness of his hair
and the child's sunburn on his smooth brown
skin . . . replaced by desire, pure and simple. *If
you looked into my eyes right now,* she thought,
you'd know . . .

She sighed and fixed her gaze on Dumbo Williams.

After an endless pause, his voice returned, a
whisper. "Will you stop staring at that damn
horse and look at me?"

Stevie turned her head slowly, looking down at
him with heated blue eyes. He was smiling, but
the smile was preoccupied. He lifted his hand, his
fingertips drawing a feather-light pattern on her
neck. Her heart sprinted. "What do you want?"
she whispered.

His eyes were drowsy with frustrated longing.
"A fair chance."

Stevie's lips parted on a breath, knowing how
close she was to giving him that chance. Her
hand moved uncertainly to his hair, fingers tangling in the heavy strands. Her palms felt so hot,
his silky hair so cool. She stroked and lifted it,
mesmerized by the way it fell across his forehead,
her eyes caught by the highlights of copper and
gold. Her mouth was dry; she wet her lips with

the tip of her tongue. He was so still, so... patient, staring at her with hungry eyes and demanding nothing. Everything within her was tensing, ready to offer... something, anything.

He lifted his hand and slowly crooked his finger, beckoning. Asking. Time stilled while she waited, her eyes drifting helplessly down to his mouth. And then she leaned forward, so slowly, brushing his lips with hers. It wasn't a kiss, but more of an exploration—cool satin and hot silk, touching with breathless hesitation. Desire shivered through her, filling her with a delight so strong she had to smile against his lips. A simple touch had never given so much.

Mick's arms circled her, bringing her gently down to him. Still he held back, the kiss no deeper than a sigh. He had all the time in the world, and there were so many answers to find. The taste of her mouth. The shape of her lips, warm and willing against his. The flow of her breath when her heartbeat quickened and the passion rose steadily...

His body shifted instinctively, rolling, partially covering hers. Desire prickled with heat up and down the length of his body. He could feel the spontaneous arching of her back, the movement pressing her breasts against his chest. His fingers tangled into her hair, drawing her into the kiss with a growing abandon. His tongue touched the inside of her mouth and hungers he had never dreamed of washed over him in waves. They kissed in lost ways, their mouths moving against each other's, their bodies brushing soft sound from the quilt. Playful and hungry, serious and stinging, setting themselves free to play like kittens until it was no longer a game. His hands moved with a quiet desperation, stroking her back, her sides, finally moving beneath the soft knit top to the fullness of her breasts. When his thumbs discovered her taut nipples, she whimpered against his mouth, her fingers digging into his shoulders. His heart felt like it was choking him and the sun was hot on his back.

She took a shaky breath and tried to turn her head. He was acutely sensitive to everything she did, even so slight a movement. He pulled back, staring at her long and hard, the sweet wonder of pleasure lighting his eyes. *I could love you,* he thought. *I could love you, Stevie.*

"Thank you," he said softly, a shaky smile fanning across his lips.

Stevie looked at him with soft-sad eyes, because she knew that sanity was returning. It had been so wonderful to forget, even for a moment, how dangerous this was. She took a deep breath, trying to slow the staccato rhythm of her heart. "Thank you for what?"

"My chance," he said simply. His body was aching, his mind frantic with the pressure to say the right thing. Instinct told him she needed more time. A moment of thick silence passed before he said, "I would never hurt you."

"I know," she whispered. But the quiet shadows in her eyes still doubted.

The briefest flicker of disappointment tightened his features. Then he smiled reassuringly, catching her hands and pulling her to her feet. "We're corrupting Dumbo Williams," he said lightly. "It's time I took you home."

He returned her to her doorstep in the rainbow blaze of a setting sun. It was a touchy moment, feeling as he did and seeing the lingering desire in her hot bluebell eyes. He kissed her once, a brief, desperate kiss that they both broke from flushed and trembling. Then he touched his fingertips to her trembling lips, whispered, "Good night," and left her.

There was a bay window in Stevie's bedroom, overlooking, appropriately enough, San Diego Bay. The window seat was overflowing with dozens of pillows, large and small, soft and lacy, a cocoon of comfort on those scary days in life when she wasn't quite sure what came next. After Mick Connover left her with his kiss still vivid on her mouth, she felt desperately in need of comfort and warmth. Shivering, she headed straight to her window seat and burrowed in, covering herself with pillows. She was still cold. She would gladly have traded four dozen pillows for Mick Connover's arms.

Why not? she asked herself a thousand times. Why not Mick? It had been years since she had allowed herself to love a man. There had been someone a long time ago, when she had first come to San Diego. She had been "finding herself," willy-nilly, drunk with the freedom to be who and what she chose. She had thrown herself into a passionate affair that was more a declaration of independence than of love. Naturally she had chosen a brooding college student her parents would have thoroughly disapproved of. The affair had been short-lived, and her shiny new courage had suffered a few nasty bruises.

Since that time, she'd come full circle. She had *become* herself, and she had gloried in the unmistakable freedom of permanent change. And now she wanted more. She wanted to believe every word Mick Connover said to her. She was vaguely conscious of a sort of teetering happiness, a heart-in-the-throat anticipation that nearly outweighed the torments a relationship with a man like Mick Connover could cause.

I'd never hurt you.

She sat in the window seat until the room turned dark and the lights flickered brightly in the Bay. She sat until her legs were bloodless and her feet were tingling and still she was no closer to an answer. Eventually hunger pains drove her from her warm little pocket. She fixed herself a light meal and took a long hot shower. She was too tired to slather on the night creams. She went to bed with a naked face and a permanent frown etched between her brow.

It could only have been fifteen or twenty minutes later when the phone rang. Eyes closed, Stevie fumbled for the receiver, knocking it off the bedside table. She chased it halfway under the bed before she finally caught it.

"Slippery little devil," she mumbled by way of greeting, flopping back on the bed.

"Happy birthday to you, happy birthday to you, happy birthday dear Stevie, happy birthday to you."

Morgan. Birthday. Her eyes flew open and she saw what she had missed before—sunlight. "It's my birthday," she said in the same tone she would have used to say, My house is on fire.

"Well, of course it's your birthday," Morgan said heartily. "Your *thirtieth* birthday, pumpkin. You sound awfully foggy. Are you going senile already, or did I wake you up?"

Stevie knuckled her thirty-year-old eyelids. "You woke me up."

"How can that be?" Morgan boomed. "It's nearly ten o'clock in the morning. You should be out celebrating. Surely there's something an older person could do for entertainment . . ."

Stevie slipped down in the bed until the tip of her nose was hidden in the covers. "I think I hate you."

Morgan was undeterred. Morgan was *always* undeterred. "Would you like me to come over and help you celebrate? We could go to the park and feed the pigeons. That's quite a popular activity among the older generation."

"You should know, buddy. You're four years older than I am."

"That was a low blow," he said, wounded.

"Besides, men don't age like women do. They just get distinguished. Listen, I want to come over and give you your present, but I haven't bought it yet. Are you going to be around later?"

"Please don't buy me a present, Morgan. I have absolutely nothing to celebrate."

Happily, "All right, I won't. But I will come over and bring you a cupcake and wish you happy birthday in person. Do you think I can get thirty candles on a cupcake?"

"I'm sure you'll try." Stevie knew he was just trying to cheer her up in his own unique and thoroughly obnoxious fashion. Normally it worked. Today was an exception.

"Yes, I will. You know, you shouldn't be so touchy about this. You look very good for an older woman."

Stevie hung up on him without a qualm.

She went to the bathroom, fortifying herself with a vigorous dousing of cold water. Astringent. Lotion. More lotion. A heavier application of makeup than usual, though she didn't examine her motivation too closely. She was determined to pass this day like any other day, which it wasn't. She was determined, just the same.

She dressed in khaki shorts and a white cotton blouse. She opened every window in the apartment, letting the morning breeze wash through the rooms. It was a perfect day to do something domestic, something to take her mind off the big bad "B" word.

She was cleaning out her closet when the

deliveryman knocked on the door. She was expecting him. She took the small package he gave her and put it on the coffee table in the living room, unopened. Like every other year, the present was mailed from New York, though her parents lived in Atlanta. Her mother's secretary sent a wish list to Tiffany's every year, and they in turn mailed gifts on the appropriate dates. Vaunda Knight was famous for never missing a birthday.

Stevie attacked her housework with new energy. She vacuumed beneath the sofa cushions, cleaned out the fridge, and put new shelf paper in her kitchen cabinets. She was waxing her kitchen floor when she heard Morgan's jaunty knock at the door. At that point, she realized she had waxed herself into a corner, and that corner was nowhere near the front door.

"Come in," she yelled, mentally judging the distance between her corner and the hallway. Even with a running start, she'd land smack in the middle of her freshly waxed floor. Oh, wouldn't Morgan get a kick out of this one?

But it wasn't Morgan. It was Mick Connover, dressed in white jeans, a striped cotton shirt, and a soft smile. His hair was still damp, finger-combed away from his face, and there was a tiny razor cut on his chin.

"Hello there, sweet cakes." He smiled at her easily, his eyes dancing sparks as he took in her predicament. "We've gotten ourselves into a pickle, haven't we?"

Perhaps everyone went through this sort of thing on their thirtieth birthday, Stevie thought dispiritedly. Depression. Humiliation. "I guess it's just one of those days," she said, managing a faint smile. It felt like dried mud on her face.

"You must take your waxing very seriously." Mick studied her thoughtfully, one lean hip resting against the door frame. She looked terrific in shorts, but the blues didn't suit her at all. "I've never seen you look quite so . . . discouraged."

Stevie shrugged, avoiding his eyes. "It takes a special kind of genius to wax herself into a corner."

"You have to keep these things in perspective." His tone was light, deliberately playful. "If it's going to plunge you into a depression, I'd say stomp across the wet floor and to hell with it." A dazzling smile here. "But that's just my opinion."

"I just spent an hour waxing this floor," Stevie said, "and I'm not going to stomp across it." She leaned her mop against the wall and sat down in the corner, looping her arms over her bare knees. "I figure I'll be a free woman in about fifteen minutes."

So, Mick thought. It was a sit in. He shrugged and sank to the floor with easy grace, hands folded neatly in his lap. "So we'll talk for fifteen minutes," he said. "By the way, it's good to see you."

The husky tone of his voice sent nervous shivers running through her. She swallowed hard. "Even if you have to sit in the hall?"

"Even so." His wayward mouth held a curious smile. "Do you know your house smells very fresh and clean?"

"I've been cleaning."

"*And* waxing?" He raised one dark brow. "Aren't you the busy bee?"

"I like to keep busy," she muttered.

He looked at her for a long moment. Then he said peacefully, "I hate secrets. They drive me crazy. If you knew me better, you would realize how futile it is to try to keep secrets from me."

"I'm not keeping any—"

He smiled. "Yes, you are. You're filling your apartment with toxic fumes, you're waxing yourself into corners, and you haven't given me a real smile since I got here. Why?"

It was a ridiculous way to have a conversation, sitting on the floor with a wax slick between them, voices raised to carry from the hallway to the kitchen. Stevie looked at the way his long legs were folded up beneath him and her mouth quirked at the corner. "Because."

"Now we're getting somewhere. Because why?"

"Because..." She took a deep breath, dropping her chin on her knees. "Because it's my birthday."

He considered this for a moment. "I didn't wax the floor on my birthday."

"This is special." Her tone implied anything but. "The tenth anniversary of my twentieth birthday." Then, when he looked at her blankly, "I'm *thirty*, Mick."

His first impulse was to laugh. Looking at the expression on Stevie's face, Mick thought better of it. "Happy birthday," he said automatically.

"Oh, please."

He shrugged helplessly. "I really don't understand why it should get you down. So you're thirty. Why should that make you unhappy? Yesterday you were twenty-nine and eating peanut butter sandwiches and watering the flowers in my garden and enjoying yourself thoroughly. Is there really that much of a difference in twenty-four hours?"

"Are you trying to tell me it didn't bother you when you turned thirty?" she demanded.

He looked at her silently. It occurred to him that she wasn't the only one who was trapped in a corner. Finally he shook his head. "I haven't had a problem with that," he said slowly. "Not . . . yet."

At least half a minute passed before she could speak. Then she brought her hands to her temples, as if trying to soothe a raging headache. "How old are you, Mick?" she asked huskily.

If you laugh, Connover, she's likely to skewer you with a mop. "I'll be twenty-nine on my next birthday."

"Which is . . . ?"

He sighed heavily. "Eleven months. Are you going to have a problem with this, sweet cakes?"

She gave him a smile that wasn't a smile. "Yes,

I am going to have a problem with this. I can tell you unequivocally that I'm going to have a problem with this."

"You just need a little time to adjust."

"I'm old enough to be your mother."

The laughter came then, and there was nothing he could do to stop it. Each time he tried to get himself under control, one look at her stony expression would set him off again. In the middle of it, he gasped out, "Do you think the floor is dry yet?"

"What?"

"The floor. I just wondered if it was dry." He stood up, trying to discipline his Silly-Putty smile. "It doesn't really matter. Ready or not, here I come."

He left six perfect sneaker prints on her sticky floor. He pulled her to her feet and into his arms in one smooth gesture, bringing his mouth down hard over hers. She melted against him in a seizure of need, welcoming the hard lines of his body, her senses hungry for the taste and feel of him. Her hands winnowed into his damp, sunstreaked hair, her belly strained against his. This was what she wanted, what she had been missing for twenty-four long, empty hours. This was what she had tried to relive sitting alone in her bedroom, staring at the stars.

Mick had intended to take control of the situation; instead he lost it. His body burned, and he hated the small voice that whispered caution. He stroked her curves hungrily, his tongue exploring the sweet taste of her mouth, savoring. Her response told him all the things she was afraid to put into words. He asked and she answered, and he knew that it was only a matter of time.

He tore his mouth from hers, staring into the unguarded storm of her eyes. He'd been so long without this woman, so many days and nights searching strangers' faces, wondering when and if he would find her. Now that he could hold her in his arms and in his eyes, he was overwhelmed with shaky, hot elation. His heart was beating fast and hard; he felt like he was twelve years old again and had just discovered his shiny red bicycle on Christmas morning. He played that back in his thoughts and smiled to himself. Truly he had the soul of a poet.

"You have no idea—" He paused, taking in a betraying breath. "You have no idea how grateful I am."

Her eyes were very wide. "Grateful?"

"Uh-hum. Grateful I found you." A soft smile. His unsteady fingers rested for a moment on her cheek. "I was getting a little worried in my old age. I was afraid I'd have to muddle through life without you."

Stevie was quiet, a strange tightness in her throat. The level of simple honesty in Mick Connover was terrifying...and touching. Unvarnished sincerity...whatever would the man come up with next? She smiled, or tried to. "If I were you, I wouldn't mention old age. Not on my birthday."

"Actually I was trying to distract you from your birthday," he said hopefully. He trusted himself to leave only the briefest of kisses on her forehead. "How am I doing?"

"Making progress," she said with a sigh. And he was.

He smiled, smoothing the hair behind her ear with a gentle touch. "I've only just begun."

"Oh?" Her voice cracked in the middle of the word, making it sound more like, "oh-oh."

"I have plans. You can't spend the rest of the day up to your ankles in floor wax, especially if it's your—"

"Watch it."

"—if it's the tenth anniversary of your twentieth birthday," he amended, wide-eyed and innocent. "Come outside and play with me."

"I don't know. I was going to grout my bathroom tile this afternoon." There was a reluctant smile in her voice.

"Why don't you save that for next Sunday? It'll give you something to look forward to."

"You have a point." Like Cinderella, she was being sprung. Excitement and anticipation suddenly transformed the day into a golden promise. She could waste time and energy fighting her feelings, but it wouldn't change the facts. Quite possibly she would regret letting her guard down. Quite possibly she didn't care. "I'll go," she said, her eyes bright as sequins. "Give me five minutes to fix my hair—"

"Waste of time," he said, pulling her along beside him. The rubber soles of their shoes turned into velcro on the fresh wax. "I brought the Jeep, and the top's down again."

"Where are we going?"

He smiled over his shoulder. "To Camp San Diego."

Chapter
6

WHILE THE WIND WHIPPED through the Jeep and
tossed her hair like a salad, Stevie mused over
their destination. Camp San Diego. It sounded
like a spa, one of those terribly chic places with
German masseurs and papaya body wraps and
flotation therapy. It certainly didn't sound like
Mick Connover.

"Is it really a camp?" she asked at a stoplight,
when she could talk without shouting.

"No."

She had an alarming thought. She looked
down at her shorts and sandals and back to Mick.
"It isn't a private club, is it?"

"No." A smile nudged the corners of his lips.
"Nosey, aren't you? Green light. Hang on, sweet

101

cakes, Camp San Diego is just around the corner."

He pulled up in front of a two-story wood-sided building with a covered redwood porch and white shutters. A polished oak sign over the door proclaimed CAMP SAN DIEGO. It must have been a charming house thirty or forty years earlier, inspiring visions of lush gardens and elaborate wrought-iron fences. The rising value of commercial property near the harbor had replaced the fences with parking lots and the flower beds with concrete. Although most of the houses on the street had been torn down and replaced with strip malls and anonymous office buildings, a few had been restored and converted into specialty shops. Camp San Diego was nestled snugly between Toby's Tobacco Emporium and The Bayside Art Gallery.

Mick helped her from the Jeep with an outstretched hand and a courtly bow. "You have arrived, Madam. Camp San Diego."

Stevie shaded her eyes against the glare of the sun, trying to see into the windows. "What is it? A store?"

"Bite your tongue," he admonished, leading her by the hand up the redwood steps. "This is not just *a* store. This is *my* store. And although we are closed to the general public on Sunday afternoon, I'm going to make an exception for you."

"You sell snowshoes!" Stevie exclaimed, getting her first good look at the display windows.

"Snowshoes in San Diego? And ropes, and tents, and bicycle helmets . . . and *electric socks*?"

"Step inside." Mick unlocked the door and pushed it open. "Peruse at your leisure. Camp San Diego is a treasure chest of answers."

"Answers to what?"

His smile deepened as he ushered her inside. "Me."

In her younger days, Stephanie Elizabeth Knight had visited the most exclusive camps in America and abroad. Never, *ever* had she enjoyed one so much as she did Camp San Diego.

She spent a full hour exploring the first floor. Mick followed her dutifully, like an attentive salesman should. She tried on sweat suits and sheepskin booties. She rode a twelve hundred dollar mountain bike around and around a jogging trampoline. She tried on a pair of electric socks and cooked her pink tootsies. She allowed the helpful salesman to fit her with skis, poles, and boots totaling well over a thousand dollars, then sighed and asked if he had a layaway program.

His smile went through her like flickering heat. "Upstairs," he said sweetly.

She looked at the loft above them, pursing her lips thoughtfully. "Your layaway program is upstairs?"

"Yes, ma'am."

She wriggled her way out of the ski boots and climbed the stairs in stockinged feet, shadowed by her devoted salesman. The loft was filled with tents of every size and shape—round tents, pointed tents, square tents, and squatty tents, all rippling and billowing in the soft breeze from the air conditioner. Camp San Diego's layaway program.

"Feel free to explore," Mick said in his most professional manner. "I'm sure you'll recognize the superior quality of the products we carry. We have camping equipment suitable for the mildest weather, as well as for sub-zero temperatures. We also carry tents specifically designed for backpackers, extremely lightweight and compact. Are you a backpacker, ma'am?"

"I'm afraid not," Stevie said, wandering through the maze of nylon and canvas. "Although your tents are very cute."

"Cute," Mick repeated in a pained voice. "Ma'am, have you ever been camping before?"

"Certainly. I spent an entire summer at the La Nichees Camp for Young Women. I also attended St. Catherine's Island Retreat, the Northridge Summer Camp, and Wentworth's Girls Village."

He stood back, watching her. She had no idea how she looked to him, her hair loose and shining in the fluorescent light, her thumbs looped in her pockets, her movements graceful and feminine. Her beautiful blue eyes were glittering with a carefully suppressed excitement that triggered a powerful sexual response inside him. The general public would be such a letdown after serving Stevie Knight. "You're familiar with tents, then," he said huskily.

"Mercy me, no." She smiled and shook her head, rocking up and down on her bare toes. "I slept in cabins, dormitories, and chalets. I've never even been inside a tent."

Well, what did I expect? Mick thought. The sun and the moon *and* the stars? She's bright and gorgeous and personable, not to mention incredibly sexy. Fortunately, she's also a good sport. She'll learn to love the outdoors, no doubt about it. "You'd like camping," he said.

"You mean with bugs and bears and such?" She lifted a flap of a two-man dome tent and peered inside. "I think not."

Mick started after her, intent on making his point. "Of course not with bears and bugs. That's why you have good equipment, so you can enjoy nature without . . . bugs and bears."

"I like picnics," Stevie said firmly. "I like walking in the moonlight on the beach. I like sitting by a fire when the fire is in a fireplace. I like sleeping on a nice soft mattress with a nice fluffy feather pillow. There is nothing even remotely appealing about sleeping on the ground in a tent."

"Have you ever done it?" Mick demanded.

Her smile got bigger. "Not once."

"Then how do you know you wouldn't like it?"

"Elementary, dear Watson." She tossed her hair over one shoulder in a glossy fall. "The

ground is hard and cold, a bed is soft and warm.
Silly man. How on earth do you ever convince
people to spend money on a tent? There's absolutely nothing to recommend it."

"Do you see the large tent at the far end of the
room?"

"The yellow one? Yes. It's very pretty."

"I'll meet you there in three minutes."

He went back downstairs, muttering something about bugs and bears. Stevie's eyes took in
light as she watched him go, her smile carrying a
wealth of tenderness. Obviously it was very important to him that she enjoy the things in life
that gave him pleasure. She was touched, though
she couldn't muster a great deal of enthusiasm
for sleeping on dirt with only a little silk wall to
shield her from The Great Outdoors, and all the
beasts and crawly things therein. She wasn't convinced, but she was touched.

There were wire book racks on the far wall
near the yellow tent. She went to them, pulling
out several paperbacks at random. *Alaska Bear
Tales. A Climbing Guide To Mexico's Volcanoes.
Trout Magic. Kayaks to Hell. Bushwalking in
Papua, New Guinea.* Giggling, she took the
books to the yellow tent and ducked inside. She
was perfectly willing to spend a few moments
with a tent over her head, particularly if she had
interesting reading material.

She was thumbing through *Kayaks to Hell*
when Mick threw open the front flap. "There you

are," he said. "For a minute I thought you'd run off on me."

"I'm having a tenting experience," Stevie replied serenely, peering at him over the top of the book. "I'm an open-minded woman, and I'm never above trying new things. I'll thank you to zip that little mesh door shut so the bugs don't get in."

He grinned and tossed something white and fluffy at her. "I like an adventurous woman. Here, spread this out on the floor."

It looked like a very large, very flat rabbit. "What is it?" Stevie asked, coming out of her book for a closer inspection.

"It's called a Kozy Krow," Mick said patiently. "New Zealand's Premier Wool Sleeper. Look on it as a sheepskin mattress. The manufacturer guarantees ninety days of better sleep, or your money back."

Stevie smoothed out the sheepskin over the floor of the tent. It felt incredibly thick and warm, cushioning her little yellow burrow in cloudy softness. "This is fantastic. Who invented this thing?"

"Sheep," Mick said. A sausage-shaped bundle sailed into the tent, bouncing against her knees. "Now roll that out. It's a sleeping bag, in case you don't recognize it, filled with downy little goose feathers. *Then* tell me you're never going to sleep in a tent."

She did as she was told, pulling the sleeping bag out of the nylon duffel and positioning it neatly in the center of the tent. While she worked, she appreciated the white denim fantasy framed in the square mesh door. Incredible legs. Muscular thighs. Lean hips and flat stomach. Above that, the tent took over. Stevie's palms began to sweat. "All right," she said huskily, "I've rolled it out. And I'm never going to sleep in a tent."

Immediately he went down on one knee, frowning through the white mesh. "Why do you say that? Aren't you comfortable?"

"Perfectly." She stretched out on her side on top of the sleeping bag. "Warm and soft and cozy. I feel like I'm on a cloud."

"Then why did you say you wouldn't—"

"Because you told me to say it." Her smile was a symphony. "*Stoopid.*"

He grinned, much relieved. He ducked inside the tent, then turned and carefully zipped the flap shut. "No bugs," he said solemnly. He sat down, Indian style, rubbing his palms over the thick white pile. "Now tell me the truth. A sinfully comfortable bed. Fresh mountain air. All the stars in the heavens drifting down around you like snowflakes. Can you imagine anything more restful?"

He was awfully close. His voice seemed an octave lower in the closed space, warm and rich, playing with her senses. His classically sculpted cheekbones softened in the faint golden cast from the tent, his eyes brighter, more diffuse. "You're very persistent," she said softly. "Something tells me you won't rest until you make me a nature lover."

"I never make anyone do anything." His dark eyes were serious, though he smiled. "I just let them know how I feel, and leave the decisions up to them."

He wasn't talking about camping, and they both knew it. Stevie sat up abruptly, reaching for the books in the corner of the tent. "Look what I found . . . the most interesting reading material. Take this for instance." She held up *Bushwalking in Papua, New Guinea.* "Not everyone has this little number on their coffee table at home, you know."

"They should," Mick said thoughtfully. "It's a fantastic book. I wouldn't have enjoyed New Guinea nearly as much if I hadn't read it first."

"You've been to New Guinea?"

He nodded. "Last year."

"And you went . . . *bushwalking*?"

"Yes, I went . . . *bushwalking*," he said, mimicking her wide-eyed fascination. "Is that so incredible?"

Stevie found it more than incredible. In her experience, men with Mick Connover's background were far more familiar with the casinos of Monte Carlo than the bush country of New Guinea. "Believe it or not, most people don't spend their summer vacations in Papua. Most people have never even heard of Papua."

"Their loss," he said cheerfully. "What else do you have there?"

"*Kayaks to Hell*," she said. "Have you ever . . . ?"

"Not to hell." The air he breathed was sweetened with her scent. It drifted over his clothes, his skin, surrounding him. "Just down the Colorado."

A little smile passed over her mouth. "Of course. Just down the Colorado. What about Alaska?"

"What about Alaska?"

"Have you been there?"

"A couple of times. I went with a friend, a biologist, to the Pribilof Islands to study the fur seals one summer. Actually, he did all the studying. I just enjoyed the scenery. And once I went to the North American Championship sled-dog races in Fairbanks. That was three or four years ago."

"How do you think of these things?" Stevie asked in amazement. "New Guinea, the Pribilof Islands, sled-dog races . . ."

"Elementary, my dear Watson." He smiled and patted her cheek. "I'd never been to New Guinea. I'd never met a fur seal up close and personal. Never once had I seen a sled-dog race. Can you imagine how many questions I had? Naturally I needed answers."

"Naturally." Mick Connover had promised her a few answers of her own today, and she hadn't been disappointed. He was a gentle man, far more interested in discovering the world around him than conquering it. And somehow that made him stronger, more appealing, than any man she had ever known. "*His life was gentle,*" she said softly, "*and the elements so mixed in him that Nature might stand up and say to all the world 'This was a man.'*"

"That wasn't from *Kayaks to Hell*," Mick said, the faintest edge of embarrassment in his voice.

"No, it wasn't. Julius Caesar, Act Five." She was quiet then, letting her gaze play over the endearing flush on his cheeks, the wry smile on his lips. And she watched his hands as they moved absently over the sheepskin, fingers curling into the thick pile. He enjoyed touching things, she thought, absorbing shapes and textures. She thought of the soft expression in his eyes when he'd touched her skin, the way he had stroked his palm over her hair. Quietly finding his answers. He caught her staring at his hands and he stilled them abruptly, his mouth quirking self-consciously. She smiled. "I think I like you, Mick Connover."

He leaned forward, resting his hands lightly on her shoulders. His voice was as soft and unhurried as hers had been. "I think I like you too, Stevie Knight." He drew her to him by inches, his eyes sweetly drowsy, his lips settling over hers in a swirling kiss. Slowly, slowly . . . with tenderness and reverence and devastating eroticism. He wanted to make the kiss gentle and long-lasting, but there was no way he could do one along with the other. He knew his limits. He raised his head, his breath coming in quiet little shocks. He smiled at her, the wide mouth hypnotically sensual. Huskily he said, "I think it's time I took you to Heaven."

"Heaven?"

"I've been craving a Taste of Heaven ever since the night you kidnapped me. Passion Fruit with chocolate topping." He was trying to maintain his cool, but the moist, baby-curves of her mouth distracted him. He took a quick breath, then kissed her hard, and released her. "Where was I?"

"Heaven," Stevie said hoarsely.

"Was I ever," he murmured. Then, getting back to business, "Since I was blindfolded that night, I haven't had much luck finding the place. Do you think if I said please, you'd give me the address?"

She could feel the crooked curve of her own smile. "Maybe. I kind of hate to leave my tent, though."

His eyes delivered a tidy little message: *You'd better.*

"Sixteen East Camden," she said.

Unfortunately, Heaven was closed on Sunday. They settled for a fast food picnic on a grassy bluff above the beach. The sun had dropped out of sight, but the sky and the water still held a gentle reflective glow. This was Stevie's favorite time, that quiet deep blue hour between day and night.

"What do you think this is called?" she said softly.

Mick glanced at the hamburger she held. "A Big Mac. No, wait . . . that's a quarter pounder. I had the Big Mac."

She shot him an amused glance beneath heavy lashes. "Not the food, Mick . . . this time of day. What do you think it's called?"

"Oh." He gave the matter thirty seconds of careful consideration while he finished off his hamburger. "Sunset."

"Look around, Michael James. Do you see a sun that's setting?"

"Well . . . no." He looked out toward the sea, the wind whipping his straight hair about his head. "The sun has already set. Or sat, as the case may be."

"Then it couldn't be sunset," Stevie said, watching him as he watched the sea. His dark eyes were narrowed against the dull reflection of the water, giving him a dreamy, preoccupied look. "So here it is, M. J. Connover, one of those questions you just love to find answers for. What do you call this glorious pause between day and night?"

"Almost-night." He turned his head, gifting her with a breathtaking smile. "When I can't find answers, I make them up. That way I'm never frustrated."

Stevie returned his smile, tit for tat. "Never?"

"Almost never." The gentle amusement slowly faded from his eyes. He lifted his hand, slowly letting his fingers whisper over the arch of her cheek, feeling the soft warmth. She sighed; his little finger dropped to parted lips, tracing the sweet curves that haunted his dreams. "Sometimes I have trouble on Sundays," he whispered. "Especially during almost-night."

Stevie's eyes drifted closed, absorbing the searing tenderness in his voice. "Do you know how I deal with frustration?" she asked against his fingers.

"No." His fingertip barely entered her mouth, touching the cool silk interior, spreading the moisture over her wind-dried lower lip. "How do you deal with frustration?"

It took her a moment to remember. Ah, yes. "I exercise," she said, jumping to her feet. "I'll race you to the parking lot, Connover!"

Jumping over the grassy hillocks, laughing in the wind, she reached the parking lot a good five seconds ahead of him. He caught her as she was climbing into the Jeep, turning her in his arms and holding her a few inches above the ground. His eyes were lit with excitement and contentment, crinkled with a lifetime of smiles. "Don't smirk," he ordered. "You only won because I stopped to throw the garbage away."

"I won because I'm faster," she said breathlessly, her sandals dropping off her feet. "You couldn't even touch me."

He lowered her by inches, sensual heat shivering down his spine from the brush of her body. "Sure about that?" he drawled softly.

Her heart was pounding wildly. It was hard to catch her breath, hard to still the trembling in her suddenly tender muscles. "You're going to strain something. Put me down."

"You're not exactly a romantic, are you?"

"Please?"

He lowered her into her sandals with neat precision and a wry smile. "Your wish is my command," he said. He looked up at the sky, finding the first blurry star in the darkness. "Almost-night is over. It doesn't last long, does it?"

"No, it doesn't." A vague sense of loss drifted down, surrounding her. She sighed and immediately Mick turned his head, watching her. Reading her.

"Maybe you are a romantic, after all." His smile was tender, reaching deep into his eyes. The wind pulled her hair across her face, and he tucked it gently behind her ear. "Sweet girl," he whispered, "I never want to say good-bye to you."

He caught her off guard. He said words that sent her blood slapping in hot gushes through her veins, delivering them with a winsome Boy Scout smile that made her wonder if she'd heard right. And so she simply stared at him, all the questions and uncertainty there in her eyes for him to see.

He sighed, an exaggerated, long-suffering sigh that almost made her smile. Almost. "When are you going to relax and let this thing happen with us?"

"I don't know," she said helplessly.

He raised both eyebrows in teasing inquiry. "You want to take a guess?"

This time she did smile. Feelings she couldn't put into words made a hard lump in her throat.

"I suppose I should take you home," he said, when he saw she wasn't going to answer. So much was in his face: resignation, desire, a kind of brittle patience. "You're shivering. That means you're either cold or terrified. I prefer cold."

He drove home at a snail's pace to cut down the wind chill, the heater blasting full force. Night had fallen in earnest by the time they reached her apartment, and lights were glowing warmly from several windows... including the corner unit on the third floor.

"That's odd," Stevie said, never even noticing that Mick had parked illegally in front of a fire hydrant. "The lights in my apartment are on."

Mick glanced up, frowning. "Did you leave them on?"

"I don't think so." She shrugged. "Then again, maybe I did. They say the memory is the first thing to go."

"I don't think they were saying it to a thirty-year-old, sweet cakes. Come on, I'll check things out. You know how I love solving mysteries."

But there was no mystery to be solved. As soon as Stevie stepped out of the elevator on the third floor, she had her answer. "It's Morgan," she said.

Mick's brows drew together. "What's Morgan?"

"He came to visit." Smiling, she pointed to the squashed cupcake sitting on top of a white envelope in front of her door. What appeared to be dozens of little pink birthday candles were crammed into the frosting at all angles. "He said he was going to bring me a cupcake. I'd forgotten he was coming over."

"That's nice," Mick said shortly.

Stevie eyed the cupcake doubtfully. "You think so?"

"It's nice you forgot he was coming over," he qualified sweetly.

He followed her into the apartment like a shadow. Morgan was nowhere to be found, but evidence of his visit was everywhere. A newspaper was scattered over the sofa. The stereo was playing softly. The refrigerator was practically empty, and the kitchen sink was full of dirty dishes. There was a note on the kitchen table next to an empty carton of milk.

> I was here, but you weren't. I waited for a half hour and then gave up. Enjoy your cupcake. I owe you a quart of milk, two apples, and eight eggs. I made an omelet. What's in the package on the coffee table? I wanted to open it, but I didn't because it would have been rude.
>
> Happy Birthday to You!
> Morgan Nathaniel Jones

Mick read the note over Stevie's shoulder. "You mean he did all this damage in thirty minutes?"

Stevie nodded. "He's like a tornado. He never stays in one place for long, but the devastation is incredible."

And then Mick asked the one question that truly demanded an answer. "Does he just walk in and out at will?"

"He has a key," Stevie said. Mick's dark eyes narrowed and she added quickly, "This apartment used to be his. When he moved into a bigger place, I took over the lease. I keep meaning to have the locks changed, but I've never gotten around to it." She paused for a breath. "Why am I explaining all this to you?"

"Because you didn't want me to misunderstand." Mick smiled, feeling infinitely better. A little encouragement was always nice, particularly when his heart and soul were involved. "So what's in this package Morgan mentioned? You know how I feel about—"

"Answers," Stevie sighed. Beckoning with her finger, she led the way into the living room. The package was on the table right where she had left it—well, not precisely where she had left it. Morgan had obviously been fiddling with it. There were chocolate frosting fingerprints on the front. "It's from my parents," she said. "Happy birthday to me. It arrived this morning."

Mick was truly amazed. "And you didn't open

it right away? How can you stand not knowing what's in there?"

"It's easy." Stevie brushed the newspapers off the sofa and flopped down, tossing the package from hand to hand. "My parents don't even know what's in it. If they're not curious, I find it a little hard to be curious."

"I'm lost." Mick sat down beside her, crossing his arms over his chest. "I'm well and truly lost. Can we start at the beginning?"

"All right." She looked at the package, the coffee table, her broken thumbnail. Anywhere but at him. Talking about her background was difficult, but Mick had been right—she didn't want him to misunderstand. "My parents hire someone to hire someone to choose my birthday and Christmas presents. The only person in the world who knows what's inside this box is an employee of Tiffany's." She smiled, but only with her mouth. "It lacks a personal touch. Now Morgan's cupcake ... *that* has a personal touch, don't you think?"

"I think you should open it," Mick said softly.

She looked at him, then shrugged and opened the package. Tiffany's did a thorough job. She went through four layers of paper before she came to the blue velvet jewelry box. She opened it, holding it up for Mick to see. "It's a pin. It's very pretty, don't you think? Someone has excellent taste."

Mick was no connoisseur of fine jewelry, but the delicate diamond and sapphire pin had to have been worth a great deal of money. "It's beautiful," he said quietly.

"I'll write them a thank-you note tomorrow." She closed the box with a snap and put it on the table. She'd never touched the pin itself, Mick noticed. As a matter of fact, she'd been careful *not* to touch it.

"Tell me about your family," he said.

Stevie's eyes held Mick's. She smiled faintly and shrugged. "I just did."

Perhaps she was right, he thought. Perhaps he had all the answers he needed. He wasn't crazy about the story, but he'd heard it before. It wasn't uncommon in the rarefied atmosphere of the very rich. Money bred power and power bred callousness. It was a nasty circle, and she'd grown up smack dab in the empty middle of it. No wonder she was wary of his background.

Her hand was resting on the sofa cushion between them. He put his hand over it, his fingers threading through hers. "If I'd brought you a cupcake," he said softly, "I would have damn well stayed around and given it to you in person. And if I'd bought you a pin, I would have wrapped it myself and tried to make the ends of the ribbon curl like they do in the stores. Usually I just end up shredding it, but it's the thought that counts." His gaze lifted from their joined hands and fixed on her face. "Don't you think?"

Stevie nodded. She'd never been more fascinated by his eyes, by the rich, warm color, by the gravity beneath the flickering golden highlights.

He was looking at her in a way she'd seen before —part heat, part tenderness. His beautiful mouth was lazily tipping at the corners in That Smile.

"I wish you'd kiss me," she said. Then, with a flash of inspiration, "Never mind. I'm a big girl. I'll kiss you."

The sudden spark in his eyes said yes. Please, please...

She leaned forward, opening her lips to him, artless and daring and craving. The best kisses, the sweetest kisses...she spread her hands on his chest, where she could feel his heart pounding through her. Her pulse kept matching time, hard and fast. He pulled her onto his lap, his hands strong and warm at her waist. She stirred restlessly against him, hungry to find all the ways she could fit against his skin. His fingers curved over her bottom, gathering her into his hands, pressing her against him. She felt the answering shocks deep within her body. She loved the way he held her, so fierce and so gentle. She loved the dark honey hair that tumbled over his forehead, begging for her touch. She loved his sighs and his smiles and the dark eyes that talked to her. Love ran through her, warm and bright...

He turned his head, burying his lips in the satin curve of her neck. Her hair drifted over him, cooling his skin, surrounding him with a fragrance of flowers and sweet night air.

"Is this what you want?" he whispered. "You're sure now?"

She pulled away, just enough to work the buttons on her blouse. One at a time, until the material dangled open, revealing a clingy white camisole stretched tight over her breasts. "I need this," she said. Was that her voice? It didn't sound like her voice. It sounded sweet and husky and magical. A siren's voice.

He held her eyes. Slowly he ran his finger along the crocheted edge of the camisole, tickling sweet warm skin. "What do you need, Stevie? What do you want from me?"

"This. This magic we make." Her hands submerged in his thick hair, feeling it slip like water through her fingers. Her heavy-lidded eyes focused on his mouth, glazed in moisture.

His fingers spread over her breasts, cupping the aching warmth. A stab of heat marked his cheeks like a burn, contrasting with the near-black intensity of his eyes. "This is only part of what we have together," he said. "Do you understand that now?"

Stevie's hands slipped weakly to his shoulders. What did he mean? There was only the present, the here and now, and her need to give and receive pleasure. She was so full of it, there wasn't room for anything else. "Isn't this enough?" she asked, the words less than a whisper. A plea.

He looked at her, long and hard. His blood slowed, though the desire that gave him no peace remained strong and demanding. "With any other woman, it would be enough. With you . . . no. This isn't enough."

She shook her head, briefly touching her palms to her hot cheeks. "Then what? What do you want?"

For the longest time, he didn't answer. He buttoned her blouse, his fingers feeling big and awkward. Then he placed a kiss on her lips, with all the newfound tenderness in his heart. "I want..." He paused, searching for words. "I want you to want more from me. Anything else would be...unbearable for me. Do you understand?"

She moved off his lap, curling up in the corner of the sofa. Briefly she rested her forehead on her knees, then she lifted her head and looked at him curiously. "I'm not sure I understand anything anymore."

"You will." He stood, putting more distance between them, his smile fighting the burning muscles in his jaw. His body was still clamoring, questioning his ....ision. "You probably do already, somewhere beneath all your excess emotional baggage."

"My *what*?"

"Let me rephrase that." She looked so delicate to him, and yet so strong. He wanted to hold her, how he wanted to hold her. "We want the same things from each other, love. The problem is, only one of us realizes it."

"Where are you going?"

"Home," he said, grimly determined.

Her voice caught him at the door, soft and intense. "I thought all you wanted was a fair chance."

He took a deep breath, keeping his back to her. "When I leave you tonight, Stevie . . . I'm giving us a fair chance."

Chapter

7

TIME SLOWED. Monday, Tuesday, Wednesday, Thursday . . . one day following another like an indistinguishable line of squashed tomatoes. Flat. Dull. Terribly unappealing.

Morgan didn't like her anymore. He told her so on Friday when she kicked the copy machine and somehow short-circuited the power in the office.

"The damn thing was out of toner," he shouted, his eyes flashing in the sudden darkness. "Why the hell did you kick it?"

"I'm sorry."

"You should be. You've been a crazy person all week. Today it's that machine. Who knows where you'll vent your frustrations next? The computer? The water cooler? The mailman? I don't like you anymore, sweetie."

"Don't call me sweetie! I'm an adult, damn it!"

Morgan looked pointedly at the wounded copier. "Hell, yes. You're the most mature woman in this room."

Stevie looked at her watch. Fortunately, the dials were illuminated. "It's nearly four. I'm going home early."

"Oh, *would* you?" Morgan replied. "Gee, maybe by the time you come back Monday morning, you'll be sane again. I hate to sound like a broken record, but I'll give it one more shot. What's wrong with you?"

"It's personal."

"Fine. *Fine.* Have a lovely weekend wading around in your emotional swamp. I'm just glad you don't have a cat."

"Why?"

"Because if you did, you'd probably kick it." He took a deep breath and stared very seriously into her eyes. "You're angry at someone, and I don't think it's Connover. I'm perfect, so you couldn't be angry with me. Who-oh-who could it be?"

Stevie fled. She drove to the beach, Morgan's words echoing in her ears. Angry. Yes, she was angry. She was angry at Mick for saddling her with this relentless need. She was angry with Morgan for witnessing her confusion. But most of all, she was angry with herself.

She sat on the same windy overlook where she had picnicked with Mick. The breeze tugged her hair away from her face as she bent her head to study the waves below. The tension was still humming through her muscles like an electric current she didn't know how to intercept. She was tired. Avoiding the unavoidable was exhausting work.

So face the facts, sweet cakes.

No woman in her right mind would have let Mick Connover walk out of her apartment . . . or her life. He was gentle. He was honest. He had the most incredibly sexy mouth she had ever seen in her life. He grew vegetables. He gave his horse a last name. He could play a killer version of "Hey Jude" on the French horn. She trusted him, she desired him, and she needed him. So why was she sitting alone on this little mound of earth, getting grass stains on her skirt and sand between her toes?

"Because I'm a chicken," she said out loud. It was quite a relief to face the truth after dancing around it for five wretched days. She cupped her palms around her mouth, megaphone style, and shouted into the wind, "A chicken! I'm a big fat *chicken*!"

Oh, that was better. At least she knew who to blame now. Mick had been right all along. She *had* been judging him, holding back from enjoying to the fullest the happiness he had brought her way. The poor man had been born on the wrong side of the tracks, so to speak, and she hadn't been able to get past that in her mind.

She'd kept expecting ... something, anything, to justify her caution. She smiled. Thank heaven he had disappointed her time after time.

What had he said to her on her birthday? *I never make anyone do anything. I just let them know how I feel, and leave the decisions up to them.* A mature attitude. Unfortunately, he wasn't dealing with a mature woman at the time. Thirty years old, she thought ruefully, and barely ripe.

She stood up and stretched, raising her face and her hands to the sky. The sun was gone. It was almost-night. She gave it the attention it deserved, watching the smoky blue sky swallowed in the darkness. She took a deep breath, letting the rushing, rhythmic sounds of the ocean soothe her.

She wouldn't go to him tonight. She wanted just a little more time to settle all the restless thoughts, to dream the future. She didn't want to miss out on a single thing, including the anticipation. Tonight was Christmas Eve, and tomorrow...

"Merry Christmas, Mick Connover," she whispered.

His flowers were dying.

Mick couldn't figure it. He'd fertilized them up one side and down the other. He'd watered them. He'd even talked to them, pouring out his frustrations to the marigolds and the petunias. If anything, they'd drooped a little farther after his tale of woe. He didn't blame them. It was a damn sad story.

He couldn't believe she hadn't tried to contact him. He'd been at the store Monday through Friday, at home every evening with one hand on the telephone. It had been all he could do not to call and hang up, just to hear her voice answer the phone. Obviously he hadn't outgrown a few of the old junior high habits.

Saturday morning he pulled on a pair of jeans and some old rope sandals and set to work saving his foliage. It was good to keep busy. He only thought of Stevie occasionally—when he breathed in, when he breathed out. He still had hope, but it was fading quickly. Had he left her too abruptly? Had he imagined feelings that didn't exist? Had he, did he, would she, could she . . .

"Hello, stranger."

His heart bounded into his throat. He stood up slowly, a trowel in one hand, a freshly pulled dandelion in the other. Stevie smiled at him across the wilting flower patch. Hot sunlight shimmered over her, teasing delicate auburn highlights from her hair. She wore a white dress, and white sandals. And a smile that would dance through his dreams till the day he died.

"Hello yourself," he said quietly, taking her in.

"I went to the store," Stevie said, shading her eyes against the glare. She could see the sunlight and sweat that sparkled on his chest, making his brown skin glow. His hair was darkened with per-spiration, tangled over his forehead and ears. The sun caught his eyes as he looked at her, sparking hot gold from the soft brown depths. "They said you don't work on Saturdays, so I came here."

"I didn't hear your car," he said. Idiot, of course you didn't hear her car. You're in the backyard babbling to flowers, and she parked in the front. "Did you have any trouble finding the place?"

"I took a couple of lefts when I should have gone right. I stopped at a fruit stand down below and they gave me directions." She nodded, indi-cating the fluffy yellow flower he was holding. "Are you planting that?"

"What? Oh, the dandelion." He dropped it into a bucket. "No. It's a weed. I pulled it."

"Your flowers don't look too good."

"I know. I told you plants don't like me."

"Oh." This wasn't the way she had planned it. She hadn't counted on the awkward pauses. She certainly hadn't counted on the effect a low-rid-ing pair of jeans and a muscular chest could have on her vocal chords. And the trowel...the trowel could be a problem if she threw herself into his arms. His gaze was polite and unhurried, yet she found herself tensing, as if he were pres-suring her. Which he wasn't.

"I came to throw myself at you." The words came blurting out.

A smile flickered to life deep in his eyes. "Did

you?" he asked softly. She nodded, biting her lip. The smile grew, a startled curve of delight. He dropped the trowel and held out his arms.

She met him in the middle of the poor flower bed. He was laughing; he had her in his arms, holding the delicate, graceful body close against him. She scattered a rain of kisses on his jaw and chin, kisses shaped with her smile.

"We can't," he said, his mouth moving hungrily over her face even as he spoke. "I'm getting you dirty . . . I'm a mess . . . oh, you feel so good, just holding you . . ."

"I missed you." Her arms went around his neck, fierce and possessive, her palms yearning over the sun-warmed skin. Her lips found his, again and again, as if she were starved. "I need you, Mick Connover. I need you . . ."

He'd never known there was happiness like this. Standing in a blaze of heat and light, her hair spilling over his shoulders, the air as sweet as honey around them. His hand curved over her breast to absorb her heartbeat. Fast, so fast . . .

He held her tighter, as if he were holding onto a dream, and he said, "Never say good-bye to me, Stevie."

"Never," she whispered. "Never."

He picked her up in his arms, a smiling bundle that weighed less than nothing. He carried her across flowers and parched grass and into the cool shadows of the house to his bedroom, darker still because the shutters over the windows were still latched. He hadn't felt like sunlight this morning.

He placed her gently on the edge of the bed where the sheets dangled to the floor. He hadn't felt like housekeeping this morning, either.

Stevie saw the frown in his eyes. He'll never be able to keep anything from me, she thought. His eyes talk too much. "What?" she asked softly.

"It's a mess," he said, actually blushing. "The whole room. I never even made my bed."

"And what a waste of time that would have been."

He looked at her, loving her with his eyes. The wispy bits of dandelion in her hair, her smooth skin, and her beautiful white dress...smudged with dirt and fingerprints. Quite a few fingerprints.

He went down on his knees, resting his head in her lap, his arms circling her waist. She put her hand on his hair and began to stroke it. My friend, she thought, sudden tears blurring her vision. No wonder love had left her wanting up till now. She'd needed more than passion. She'd needed laughter and understanding and a man who loved flowers even when they didn't love him back. "You were right," she said softly. "The loving...it's only part of what I need from you. It's only part of what we are."

"Silly girl." His voice was muffled against her skirts. "I'm always right."

"We belong together."

He lifted his head and smiled at her. "I knew that from the beginning, Stevie-Stephanie. I've just been waiting for you to catch up with me."

"Here I am," she whispered.

He stood up and went to the window, throwing the shutters wide, lifting the glass. The room flooded with light and sweet fresh air. He smiled, standing there in a warm square of sun, looking out over his mountain. He could hardly believe Stevie was finally here with him, in this home he'd built and loved. He felt like a family with her.

"I need to shower," he said. "Promise me you won't go away."

Her eyes followed the sweet, hard curves of his body. "C'mere," she said with a smile.

"I shouldn't," he muttered, looking down at his soiled jeans. But he did, pulling her off the bed, holding her for a kiss that nearly destroyed his fine intentions. Nearly. He pulled back, his breath coming in shivers. "I'll be back."

She sighed. "And I'll be waiting."

He didn't want to let her go. His hands began to wander. "Wait right here."

"I promise." A lovely thought occurred to her. "Unless you'd like me to help?"

He closed his eyes briefly. He'd waited a lifetime for her already. His need was so strong, he didn't want to risk losing control. He stepped back, away from temptation. "No. I want to walk out and see you waiting for me. I've dreamed of it a hundred times."

She smiled. "You're lucky. I just happen to specialize in painless abductions *and* making dreams come true." She watched him unfasten his jeans as he walked into the bathroom. Her throat went dry.

She waited like a good girl until she heard the water running. Then, like a very bad girl, she quietly opened the bathroom door and looked inside. She saw clouds of steam, and a marbled glass shower door. And she saw his silhouette, lean and strong and beautiful. He put back his head under the running water, raking his fingers through his hair, his body exposed in a shadowed profile. Stevie drew a hard breath and carefully closed the door.

She was waiting on the edge of the bed when he came out, her hands folded as if in prayer in her lap. He was wearing a short terry robe belted loosely at the waist. His hair had had the benefit of a brisk towel rub, but hadn't seen a comb. He'd hurried, as promised.

He took one look at her expression and his mouth crooked in a smile. "You cheated," he said.

She nodded, wetting her lips with her tongue. "I did. I'm sorry." No, she thought. She shouldn't compound cheating with a lie. "I'm not sorry."

Softly: "What are you?"

She listened to the rough undertone in his voice, realizing he wasn't as relaxed as he looked. A dark excitement quivered through her with the knowledge. "I'm tired of waiting," she said.

He came to her then, his lips dragging over hers with devastating eroticism, contact breaking, meeting, breaking. The white dress with the smudged fingerprints had so many buttons, tiny pearls that stretched from the shadow of her breasts to below her waist. He worked them one at a time, his hands hungry on her clothing, her body. Every sweet inch of her was a revelation, the freckles on her shoulders, the tantalizing shadow between her breasts, the satin finish of her beautiful legs. She wore the same white chemise that he had seen once before, and his mouth closed over the hard point of her nipple through the lacy pattern. Suckling, teasing, blowing on the damp fabric. His dreams had never come close to reality.

He lifted his head to look into her eyes, nearly overwhelmed with the demands of his body. He counted to . . . something, he couldn't remember what. He wanted to go slowly. He wanted to remember everything.

His robe fell to the floor. His body was so beautiful to Stevie. She loved the shadowed hollows defining his muscles, the fire and steel that came beneath. And she loved the hazy smile that fell on her, warming her. Loving her.

She helped him remove the chemise. Her hands were shaking, though not from nervousness. She became caught up in the stormy colors of his eyes. There was no clothing to separate them, and no inhibitions. Through the open window, the wild blue sky seemed only inches away. It never entered her mind to close the shutters. His hands roamed over her breasts, palms lifting and caressing the aching, tender flesh. Her desire became fierce beneath his hungry touch. She leaned back in the tumbled sheets, pulling him with her, her fingers splayed out on his rib cage. His body brushed full length over hers for the first time, and she bit her lip to stifle a cry. Her breath and his came in ragged, husky sighs.

His mouth came within inches of hers and hovered there. His hands were braced on either side of her body, the muscles in his arms rippling and tense. "I love you. My beautiful lady, you feel so good against me . . ."

"Closer," she whispered, curling her index finger below his chin and drawing him to her. His body pressed down, hard and demanding against her nakedness, and every inch of skin burned to have more of him. He guided her deeper into kisses where fiery tongue strokes carried the erotic motion of love. Without conscious thought, her hips began stirring in the same primitive rhythm. This was no practiced ritual, calculated to elicit response. This was love, pure and natural, and her body followed a mindless path with sweet abandon.

His mouth left hers, drifting hot kisses down her neck, tasting and touching the hectic beat of her heart. Her belly strained against his as he kissed her breasts, gently biting and sucking with the most exquisite pressure. She felt like she was falling. Down, down, sinking into a warm pool of milk and honey...

He knew he was on the edge. Under the worship of his hands, she was enraptured, her breath breaking often, saying his name again and again in a husky whisper. His name... hearing it on her soft, swollen lips, the world falling away around them, he knew he was more welcome than he had ever been in his life.

His eyes were warm and blurred as he whispered, "How did I live without you? How did I make it through a day without you?"

She tried to answer him, but her throat was tight and stinging. "I can't... I need..."

"I know," he said thickly, his tongue riding liquid fire on her lips. "We both need, love."

Trusting and helpless, she felt his hands on her and she was losing control. But she didn't want control. She didn't want control or kindness or caution. Not any longer.

She eased herself around him, initiating a heady rhythm. Like wind calling to rain, his body answered hers and pleasure shook them both.

Never before had life flowed through him so strongly. He gave to her with all his heart, all his soul, never wanting it to end...

The sheets were gone. Probably on the floor, though Stevie didn't have the energy to raise herself to see. No matter. She was warm and safe and quietly spent. Beside her, Mick had his eyes closed, though she knew he wasn't sleeping. She was attuned to his every thought, and his every thought focused on her. She could feel it.

"You're staring," he said.

"Uh-hum." She was laying on her side, resting her head on her hand. "You have beautiful eyelashes."

His lips curved in a drowsy smile. "I'm laying here stark naked, and you're coveting my eyelashes?"

"Yes, I am." Her toes curled in the bewitching tangle of their legs. "And your ears."

"My ears?"

"They're perfect ears," she said. "Tucked nice and close to your head. My ears stick out like Dumbo Williams'."

"I've never noticed that." Clearly this was a matter that deserved his attention. He rolled over on his side, facing her, one hand lifting the hair away from her ear. "Oh. Well, they're not as bad as Dumbo's, but I wouldn't go getting any pixie haircuts."

"It's my only fault," she said sincerely.

"Then I certainly can't complain." He kissed her on the chin. "I used to have faults, but that was last year. This year I'm perfect."

"You must be so pleased." She kissed him on the chin. "Why are you laughing?"

"Because there's a part of me that feels like laughing." His eyes were bright, so bright. He arched, and his body aligned itself against hers. He rubbed his breathtaking smile in the hollow of her throat. "And there's a part of me that feels like shouting from the rooftop. And there's a part of me that feels like hiding you here in my room until the twelfth."

"The twelfth?"

"Of never, sweet cakes." Low lights kindled in his eyes as they swept lazily over her sweat-dampened flesh. Then, softly: "And there's a part of me that's afraid it's all just a dream."

There was something in his voice that caught at her heart. She passed a gentle hand over his boyishly tousled hair. "Look at me, M. J. Connover. My makeup is smeared, my lips are swollen, and I have a rash from your beard. Do I look like a dream?"

He stared at her. "Well . . . no."

She attacked him with the last surviving pillow on the bed. Flushed with laughter, they tumbled together, wrestling in a haze of joy.

Finally she said, "If this is a dream, reality is going to be a terrible letdown."

"Darling, after this, I'm afraid heaven is going to be a terrible letdown." He kissed her poor swollen lips with exquisite tenderness, feeling a pang of guilt. "So let's stay here in my little adobe thing and raise flowers and onions and have picnics with Dumbo Williams and be happy the rest of our lives."

"Don't you wish it were that easy?" she asked wistfully.

"It could be." His thumb soothed along her jaw, then slipped lower, rubbing the rosy points of her breasts. "What's to stop us?"

"Your job," she said huskily, closing her eyes. "My job. Your family. My family. The lease on my apartment. My dentist appointment on Monday. . ."

He half laughed, half sighed. "Dentist appointment. I can see I'm going to have to bring you along slowly. You still have one foot in reality."

She grinned, her toes playing eensy-weensy spider up his leg. "Not true. I have both feet on your . . . person."

"How can you do that? How can you bend your legs like that?"

"This is a dream," she reminded him. "Anything can happen in a dream. Have you got any requests?"

"One." He rolled on top of her, his arm bringing her close. "Don't ever wake me up."

Chapter

8

"HOLD PERFECTLY STILL."

"I *am* holding perfectly still."

"Your mouth's moving."

Stevie subsided into silence. Her neck was stiff, and the tip of her nose was scorched from the sun. She'd been sitting in her little white lawn chair in front of Mick's flower garden for the better part of an hour. Perfectly still. It was only eleven o'clock in the morning, but the relentless mountain sun was a far cry from the gentle valley sun. No wonder Mick's garden always looked thirsty.

"You turned your head," Mick said. "Don't look at the flowers. Look at me. I'm trying to get your nostrils right."

Immediately, Stevie felt her nose twitch. She'd

never been good at sitting for portraits. Had she
known Mick Connover dabbled in portraiture,
she never would have fallen in love with him.

"Lift up your chin a bit," he said. "No, too far,
Down a little. To the right . . . good."

He was sitting against a tree trunk, dressed in
sweat pants and a T-shirt, one long leg drawn up
to support his sketching pad. His hair was ruffled, due to several destructive forays with his
fingers. His expression was one of fierce concentration.

All right. He made an irresistible artist. She
would have fallen in love with him anyway.

"You're smiling too much," he observed. "I
want a very little smile, a Mona Lisa–type smile.
I'm going for a subtle, mysterious feeling here."

"Mona Lisa didn't wear men's jogging shorts
and an L.A. Lakers T-shirt."

"Not to worry. I'm improvising. Now you're
frowning too much. I need a little more smile."

"This is a silly way to spend a Sunday morning," Stevie mumbled through a Mona Lisa
smile. "I can't believe you woke me up at the
crack of dawn so you could *draw* me."

"Head up . . . Good. I didn't wake you up at
the crack of dawn, sweet cakes." A reminiscent
smile played over his mouth. "You woke me up,
if you'll remember. Keep your head up."

Technically speaking, she supposed he was
right. She'd opened her eyes at five-thirty A.M.
and discovered that Mick was clear over on the
other side of the bed. It was a horrible experi-

ence, and she'd needed immediate attention to recover from it. "But we went back to sleep," she said defensively.

Sparkling brown eyes met hers over the sketch pad. "Yeah. Two hours later."

"The point is, we could have slept till noon if you hadn't gotten this crazy urge to immortalize me on paper."

"I thought you'd enjoy a little change of pace," he said innocently. "We can't fritter away our lives in the bedroom, can we?"

She considered. Since throwing herself at him almost twenty-four hours ago, they had spent many hours in the bedroom. Many good productive hours. "I wouldn't call it frittering."

He disappeared behind the sketch pad. "Yes? What would you call it?"

She sniffed inelegantly. "Well, I sure as heck wouldn't call it frittering." She tipped her head forward, massaging the knots in her neck. "That's it. I can't sit like this any longer, Mick. My muscles are atrophying."

"Well, lucky for you, I'm finished." He looked up, eyebrows raised in polite inquiry. "Would you like to see it?"

"Of course I want to see it." She stood and came toward him, stretching stiff muscles and wriggling bloodless fingers. "Why didn't you tell me you were an artist?"

"Oh, I wouldn't call myself an artist," he said modestly. "Although my parents have one or two pictures displayed at home that I'm quite proud of. Here, come sit by me so you can get a good look."

"I don't think I can bring myself to sit again. I've had about all the—" She broke off in astonishment as he turned the picture for her inspection. She saw a stick figure with Orphan Annie eyes and corkscrew curls. A boomerang birdie was frozen above her, right next to an oblong sun. Stevie looked in wide-eyed disbelief. "This is it? This is what you've been drawing for the past hour?"

He nodded. "It's quite a good likeness, don't you think? I had a little trouble with your expression, but— Ouch!" This as she hit him on the head with the pad. "Does that mean you don't like it?" he asked forlornly.

The sketch book went sailing into the flower bed. The charcoal pencil stuck behind Mick's ear quickly followed. "You said your parents display your work!"

"They do. When I was in the first grade, I drew a picture of my mother. Kind of looked like the one I just did of you. She admired it tremendously. It's still hanging in her bedroom."

"You said . . . you said . . ." Her voice started to wobble around the edges. Her eyes grew bright, her shoulders shaking, an idiotically wide smile pushing at her cheeks. "You told me you were trying for a mysterious . . ." She buckled over with laughter, bracing her palms against her knees. "I can't believe you let me sit there for over an hour while you *stared* at me . . ."

"I love staring at you," he said, catching her hand and pulling her down beside him. "I could have stared at you all day. I could stare at you for the rest of my life." He grinned at the laughing, hiccupping bundle in his arms. "I just couldn't draw you."

"Head up," she mimicked with more groaning laughter. "Don't smile so much. Don't frown so much. Keep perfectly—"

He stopped her with the urgent pressure of his mouth. He had frittered away an entire hour since he had last kissed her. He was going through Stevie-withdrawal.

"Do you know how much I love you?" he whispered against her lips. "Do you know how happy I am?"

Her laughter faded, but her pulse sprinted on. "Tell me."

His smile was faint. "Once I read that no one could be truly happy, that we were all longing for a half-remembered Eden. And I believed it, because there were a thousand empty places inside of me that no one could fill. You've changed all that. Nothing else will ever come close to what I feel for you. I know we've barely begun, I know we'll make mistakes. But I'm going to make you happy, Stevie. I'm going to discover everything you need and want, and I'm going to give it to you." It was quite a speech for him, and he doubted he was any better with a flowery phrase than with a flower garden. He looked into her eyes and shrugged his shoulders, color stealing beneath his skin. "Sorry. I'm not . . . eloquent."

She enfolded him in the circle of her arms, her head resting against his chest. How she loved him, this man who gave so gracefully, so effortlessly. "You are by far the most eloquent man I have ever known, in every way."

His fingers played in her hair. There was a smile in his voice as he said, "Then stay with me forever in my little adobe thing. We'll live on love. I'll give you a bouquet of fresh flowers every day . . . with a little luck. I'll make wonderfully eloquent speeches. I'll never remind you of the whopping difference in our ages."

She punched him in the arm. "You had to do it, didn't you? A perfectly beautiful moment, and you had to go and make me laugh."

"I'm sorry. I can make another perfectly beautiful moment."

"No, you can't. You ruined it."

"I can." His eyes had become hypnotically bright. Gently he lowered her back in the soft, sweet-scented grass. "I can, Stevie-Stephanie. I can make as many beautiful moments as you would like. You specialize in kidnapping and dreams, I specialize in"—he dropped a kiss on the tip of her nose—"beautiful moments. Would you like one?"

She drew a soft gasp as his hand slipped beneath the voluminous L.A. Lakers shirt. Any lingering desire she had to laugh and be flippant transformed into something quiet and provocative. "I guess maybe I would."

"Here?" He held his body barely an inch from hers, looking down into her eyes. "Now?"

The steel blue sky spread above them. Stevie felt something dark and primitive twist inside her, hurting. Wanting. She touched the burning skin on his hard cheeks, the flush of passion that looked like a child's sunburn. She whispered, "Here and now..."

Stevie learned how to feed chickens that day. She left the door of the hutch unlatched and little baby guinea hens scattered like leaves in a brisk wind. She chased them around the yard, yelling for Mick, trying to shoo them back into the pen with a red bandanna she'd pulled from her hair. Mick came running from the vegetable garden, soft cotton jeans stained at the knees, his shirt flying around his waist. He took in the situation with water-bright eyes and twitching lips. He asked if she was practicing to be a matador and she stomped away to the shade of an avocado tree. Still grinning, Mick got down on one knee and made strange little clucking noises. The baby chicks plunged toward him with comical struts, following him like a devoted army back to the pen.

This man, Stevie thought in wonder, fascinated by the honey-colored hair lifting and tangling with the breeze. This amazing, beautiful man. The pleasure of the day lingered like laughter in his eyes, and his playful, kinetic energy radiated like the sun.

There was a mesmeric quality to his lithe, unhurried movements as he came toward her. His
body had an innate rhythm, the easy roll of his
hips capturing her imagination.

He smiled and sat down beside her in the
shade. His long legs were stretched out before
him, lean and coltish. "There's a trick to raising
chickens," he said. "You're supposed to keep
them fenced in. Otherwise, they run away from
home and you get real discouraged."

"I'll bear that in mind," Stevie murmured.
"Tell me more about raising chickens. Tell me
everything."

His long mouth tipped up at one corner.
"You're not going to get much sense out of me,
sweet cakes. Not as long as you're looking at me
like that."

"I'm lusting," Stevie confided. And then, at
his expression, she laughed and scattered a hand-
ful of grass in his hair.

Late that afternoon she watched him make
huevos revueltos con chorizo for their supper.
She wasn't familiar with the dish. She had to
practice for five minutes before she could even
say it.

"Just think of it as an omelet," Mick said,
tossing a reassuring glance at her over his
shoulder.

"I like to know what I'm eating." Stevie swiv-
eled in half circles on the bar stool, watching him
chop tomatoes. "What's the brown stuff in the
skillet?"

"Italian sausage."

"I thought this was a Mexican thing."

"All right. It's Mexican sausage. Any other questions?"

"What's the green stuff in the bowl?"

"Chopped green chillies. I'm getting the impression you don't trust me, sweet cakes."

She frowned. "No, that isn't it. I just can't quite believe that you really do all these things. You're a *Connover*, for heaven's sake. What did you do when you were growing up, sneak down to the kitchen and help the cook?"

"Sometimes. And sometimes I helped the gardeners. And once when I wanted to be *really* helpful, I climbed on top of the roof and tried to help the chimney sweep. I caught hell for trying to help the chimney sweep."

"I wasn't allowed in the kitchen," Stevie said reflectively. "We had a Romanian cook. I swear she was ten feet tall. She had a heavy accent, and when she spoke to me I could never understand her. She absolutely terrified me." She was quiet for a moment, enjoying the warmth and peace of the cozy room. "Mick? Do you mind if I ask you all kinds of personal questions?"

"I wish you would," he said. "I'd answer them just to hear your Scarlet O'Hara accent."

"Didn't your parents ever pressure you to be . . ."

"A standard issue Connover? Not really. I was spared that, thanks to Marshall. He's never wanted to do anything but follow in my father's footsteps, and he's damn good at it. I worked for the corporation for a couple of years after college, but my heart wasn't in it. No one was surprised when I broke away to open my own business." He thought for a minute, then grinned. "The chickens kind of gave them a shock, though."

"Did you ever resent Marshall?"

"I can honestly say I've never been anything but grateful to Marshall. He's taken the pressure off me. I can spend three guilt-free months wandering through New Guinea because I know he's happy as a lark playing real-life Monopoly. There's a certain balance there that my parents comfort themselves with."

"Do you know what I think?" Stevie said softly.

He turned, a smile in the clear, compelling eyes. "What do you think, Stevie-Stephanie?"

"I think you're wonderful," she said.

"A lovely sentiment."

"And I'm not really as hungry as I thought I was."

The smile reached his lips. "No?"

"No." She looked gravely into his eyes, those beautiful eyes that always understood. "I'd rather make love."

He moved the skillet off the stove. "You know . . . I'm not very hungry, either."

* * *

They fell asleep cuddling beneath the bed-clothes like drowsy kittens, hiding from the cool breeze from the open window. They hadn't meant to sleep. Almost-night was far too early to sleep. They would just close their eyes and rest for a moment in each other's arms.

The next sound Stevie heard was sleigh bells. She concentrated in her sleep. Was it Christmas? No, it wasn't sleigh bells she heard . . . it was the telephone ringing. Pleased to have identified the sound, she sank back into sleepy oblivion.

Tender fingers played through her hair pulled her back from sleep. She opened her eyes, look-ing at Mick's profile in the shadows. He was sit-ting on the edge of the bed, and he wore a pair of slacks and a white shirt. The last time she had seen him, he'd been sleeping on her shoulder and wearing only a tired smile.

"What is it?" she said huskily.

"I have to leave."

She sat up in bed, shaking the sleep-tousled hair from her face. "I heard the phone ring. Did something happen?"

"My father had a heart attack this afternoon," Mick said. "My mother just called to tell me. He's at Saint Mark's hospital."

"Oh, Mick." Stevie touched him gently on the shoulder, feeling the tension in the muscles there. "I'm so sorry. Is he going to be all right?"

"Apparently it wasn't too severe. The doctor said he was out of danger, but I want to see for myself." His eyes met hers, shimmering like obsidian in the dark room. "I'm sorry to have to leave you like this. It's not exactly the perfect end to a beautiful day, is it?"

"Don't worry about me." A whisper of mountain air swept the room, reminding Stevie of her nakedness. An hour ago it would have felt perfectly natural. But an hour ago, Mick wasn't wearing a dress shirt and silver cuff links. She pulled the sheets above her breasts and tried to smile at him. "I'm a big girl. I can make it back to the city by myself."

"Please don't leave." He clicked on the bedside lamp and glanced at the watch on his wrist. "It's only eight-thirty. If I leave now, I can be back in a couple of hours. Just go back to sleep. I'll be lying on the pillow beside you the next time you open your eyes."

She shook her head. "I should go home. When I came yesterday, I really wasn't prepared to stay the weekend. I need to be in the office early in the morning."

"I thought you were going to stay on my mountain forever," he said softly. "With me and my flowers and the wild little guinea hens. Remember?"

"I remember." A soft rustle of movement and she put her arms around his neck, holding tight, wishing she could melt into him and never have to let him go. "Just because I'm leaving doesn't mean I won't come back. Someone has to take care of your flowers."

He held himself oddly still, his face buried against the fragrant skin of her neck. "I wish you wouldn't go."

Her palm stroked the tawny silk of his hair. "I have to. Unless . . . do you need me?" She pulled back, her gaze searching his face anxiously. "Do you want me to come with you to the hospital?"

He did, oh how he did. But his father was out of danger and there was really no reason to impose on Stevie. Besides, it was hardly the time to introduce his lady love to his parents. "There's no need for you to come to the hospital. I'll be fine." A slow smile flickered over his lips. "And yes . . . I do need you. I need you desperately. Try to remember that when you leave my mountain, will you?"

"I will." It was hard to speak, her throat was so tight. In the soft lamplight his face looked heartbreakingly young. But his eyes . . . there was nothing childish in his dark, knowing eyes. "Everything's going to be all right, Mick."

"I know." He reached up to touch her face. "It has to be," he said simply.

Chapter

9

"I'M TIRED OF RUNNING all the errands," Morgan said. "We're equal partners, you should be running half the errands."

"I'm only asking you to go to the post office," Stevie said. "A short two-block walk. We don't have any stamps and the bills have to be mailed today."

"Then *you* go to the post office. The fresh air will do you good. You haven't been out of the office the entire week."

"I've been waiting for a call," Stevie mumbled.

"That's what you told me Monday morning when you made me go out for danish and coffee. Today is Wednesday and you're still waiting for the call?"

"Yes." Her eyes dared him to argue. She was in the mood for a good fight. "And I'm going to continue waiting. I told you, Mick's father had a heart attack. I'm worried about him."

"So call the hospital."

"I did," she said stiffly.

"And?"

"He's in good condition."

Morgan sat down on the edge of her desk with a heavy sigh. "But you still haven't heard from Connover, and you're going to continue to make me run all the errands until you do."

She nodded. "Or until Marcy gets back."

"Where the hell *is* that receptionist of ours? Why do we pay her if she doesn't show up for work half the time?"

Stevie buried her face in her hands. She had a headache. "She got called for jury duty, Morgan. I told you that. Several times."

Morgan debated for a moment. The look on his face was easily recognizable: *Should I or should I not interfere?*

True to form, he decided to interfere. "You cannot stay within lunging distance of a telephone twenty-four hours a day. It isn't practical. Have you tried calling Connover?"

"Of course I tried. He wasn't home last night or this morning. I called him at work and one of the salesmen told me he was on vacation for the next two weeks and couldn't be reached."

Again, Morgan's expression was eloquent. *I wish I hadn't interfered.* "I see. Then I guess I'm going to be playing gopher until he calls, huh?"

"No." Stevie stood up, grabbing her purse from the desk drawer. "You're right. This is crazy. There's a logical explanation for everything. I just have to wait till Mick calls to hear it. In the meantime, I have a business to run. I'll go to the post office and the bank. Do you want me to pick you up a hamburger while I'm out?"

"Extra pickles," he said happily. "And don't worry about the telephone. I won't let it out of my sight."

On the way to the post office, Stevie drove past the Connover Building. She stared up at the towering metal and glass structure where hundreds and hundreds of people spent their days like cliff dwellers. Her eyes traveled to the top of the building and found it obscured by sunlight. It probably continued half the way to heaven, just like the Tower of Babel. Up and up it goes, and where it stops, nobody knows . . .

Where are you, Mick?

When she returned to the office, Morgan was waiting for her with a "While You Were Out," message. "It takes a man to get things done," he said smugly, handing her the note. "And now if there's nothing else I can do for you, I'll take my hamburger outside and catch a few rays."

The message was short and sweet, informing her that Mick Connover called at 1:00 P.M. There was a number where she could call him back, followed by an extension number.

She dialed with clumsy, hurried fingers and got

what she assumed was a wrong number. An elderly woman told her she had never heard of Dick Hannover, and slammed the phone down in her ear. Stevie tried again, this time dialing with all the precision of a computer programmer.

Again a stranger's voice, but this one far younger and just a shade friendlier. "Connover Corporation."

Stevie blinked, then slowly gave the extension number. "Mr. Connover's office," intoned yet another female voice.

"I'd like to speak to Mick Connover please," Stevie said.

"I'm sorry, Mr. Connover is in conference and can't be disturbed." The secretary spoke with the smug satisfaction of a head waiter who tells you there isn't a table available in the entire restaurant. "Is there someone else who may help you?"

"I need to speak with Mr. Connover," Stevie said sharply. She had little patience with office protocol, a quirk left over from her childhood. East Germany had the Berlin Wall, her father had a dozen secretaries. They both served the same purpose. "Could you please tell him that Stevie Knight is calling?"

"I'm sorry, Mr. Connover isn't taking any calls right now. If you'll leave your name and number, I'll have him return your call."

"But I'm returning *his* call." Stevie took a deep breath as the secretary launched into another apologetic evasion. "All right," she interrupted, completely exasperated and more than a little confused. Since when did Mick have offices in the Connover Building? "Just tell Mick—Mr. Connover—that Stevie Knight *tried* to return his call. He can reach me at the office or at home. He has the numbers."

"I'm sure he'll get back to you as soon as time permits."

As soon as time permits. Those words returned to Stevie later as she sat blindly in front of the television set in her apartment. The ten o'clock news had already come and gone. She was wearing her stormy-night robe, though it wasn't stormy. She'd just felt in need of a little comfort.

Why hadn't he called her back? When had Mick Connover ever been dictated to by the clock? Every minute that passed without hearing from him increased her apprehension.

What was happening with him? She tried to tell herself that everything would be all right, tried not to let her delicate stomach know how anxious she was. She telephoned Mick's home and got no answer. She telephoned the Connover Corporation and got a recording.

She puttered around the house until nearly midnight. She made cookies, burned them and threw them away. She took a bath, bringing the phone into the bathroom. Later on she experimented with her face creams, trying the aloe vera on her cheeks and the avocado around her eyes. It made for a nice change, but it didn't distract her from her worries. Nothing distracted her.

The telephone rang just as she climbed into bed.

"Don't hang up on me," a repentant and much beloved voice said. "I deserve it, but please don't."

"I can't believe you finally called! Are you all right?" Stevie was breathing so fast she could hardly speak.

"I'm fine. Just . . . happy to hear your voice. How are you?"

"Never mind how I am. How are you? *Where* are you?"

"I'm here in the city. There's a penthouse on the top floor of the Connover Building. I've been staying here the last couple of nights." He sounded weary. "I know it's late, but I wanted to talk to you, and it's the first chance I've had. I was in a meeting all afternoon and I had to fly to San Francisco immediately after that. I just got back from the airport."

Stevie turned on the lamp by her bed, as if that might help her understand more clearly. "Did you say San Francisco?"

"Yeah. I had to meet with our attorneys up there. Look, it's all too complicated to go into over the phone, and I'm so tired I can't think straight. Do you think you could meet me for dinner on Friday?"

"Friday," Stevie repeated, disappointment dragging at her voice.

"I have to go to New York in the morning and I won't be back till Friday afternoon. I'm taking care of some business for my father."

She took a deep breath, trying to be calm. Trying to be patient. It wasn't easy when something in his voice made the inside of her throat and her mouth bone-dry and aching. "You want me to wait until Friday for my answers?"

A low, tired chuckle. "I'd have your head if you did this to me, sweet cakes," he admitted. "Well? Friday at seven? I have a late meeting that evening, so if you could meet me here at the penthouse, it would give us more time to talk."

"Just tell me . . ." *What do you want him to tell you, Stevie? Why it is you feel like a hurricane's coming, but you haven't got a raindrop to prove you right?* "Tell me how your father is," she said finally.

"He's doing fine. It was a mild attack, more of a warning to slow down than anything else. If he keeps improving, they'll release him from the hospital in a couple of days."

"That's wonderful." Another silence, interrupted on his end with a soft yawn. "I'll let you go, then. You sound like you could use some sleep."

"I'm getting old, Stevie."

"I hope so. Maybe you'll catch up with me."

"I mean it." Another yawn. "You know you're getting old when you're excited to go to bed . . . and you don't plan on doing anything but sleeping."

Stevie smiled, touching the receiver with her fingertips. "I'll see you Friday, Romeo."

"I'll leave your name with the guard at the front desk. He'll point you in the right direction."

He sounded so far, far away. Maybe the top of the Connover Building really was halfway to heaven. "All right," she said with a sigh. "Then I guess there's nothing else to say but—"

"Stop right there. Remember your promise? You're *never* going to say good-bye to me, lady. You almost blew it."

"Sweet dreams, M. J. Connover."

Stevie had no idea how to dress for dinner in a penthouse in the sky. In the end, she settled on a strikingly plain white silk jumpsuit. Her hair was fresh from the blow dryer: straight and shining. Her hands were shaking too badly to attempt braiding, twisting or crimping. She didn't know why she was having an attack of nerves, which made her more nervous still.

She parked in the underground terrace below the Connover Building, then took the express elevator to the lobby. The security guard at the front desk had eyes that looked like they could burn through a brick wall. He asked for identification; Stevie produced six credit cards, a driver's license, a monogrammed handkerchief, and a dry-cleaning receipt. He was not amused.

She took another elevator to the thirty-second floor, confronted and identified herself to yet another security guard, then was ushered down a wide, wide corridor carpeted in deep brown. At

the end of this corridor was a heavy wood-pan-
eled door flanked by two massive stone planters.

"Go right in," the guard said, opening the
door and stepping back. "Mr. Connover is downstairs in a meeting, but he said to tell you to
make yourself at home. He won't be long."

The first impression Stevie had was one of vast
loneliness. It might have been the incredible size
of the rooms, the twelve-foot ceilings, the shimmering glass walls overlooking a city of lights.

It might have been.

*You should have been here, Mick. I've walked
into too many empty rooms like this.*

She had to appreciate the decorator's flair for
high drama. The walls were covered with a
black-and-white herringbone print that pulsated
with silver light from a distance. Floor to ceiling
columns of Plexiglas and stainless steel separated
the living area from the dining room. The fur-
nishings were stark, yet elegant—black lacquered dining table, white leather sofas and
chairs. An elegantly appointed suite, Stevie
thought, and colder than a stainless steel kitchen.
She could hardly imagine Mick Connover living
within these neon walls.

"Kind of scary, isn't it?" Mick said behind her.

Stevie turned, her eyes widening as they took
in his white on white dress shirt, black-and-white
pinstripped tie, and black slacks. "Did you dress
to match the room, or is it a coincidence?"

His smile was both teasing and gently encour-
aging. "What it is, sweet cakes, is a pain in the

butt. I haven't been out of a suit for the past five days. Last night I fell asleep in a shirt and tie and boxer shorts. I miss my jeans." He looked into her eyes. "I miss you."

That was her cue, Stevie thought. At this point the heroine would throw her arms around the hero and tell him she missed him, too. Desperately.

But something stopped her. Instead she slipped off her shoes and tried to find the floor beneath the deep pile carpet with her toes. It wasn't there. "You're wallowing in luxury, M. J. Connover. It can't be good for you."

"Stevie?" he asked, pulling her to him.

Her lips parted at the faint, warm pressure of his. Her hands went to his shoulders, smoothing over cool silk. Suddenly her senses played back another kiss, a frantic moment on a hot Sunday afternoon, when the skin beneath her palms was sun-warmed and moist with perspiration.

Mick lifted his head, letting out his breath in a soft sound. "What is it? What's bothering you?"

"Nothing at all," she said, hoping the lie sounded better to him than it did to her. "It's just . . . been a while, that's all."

His finger tipped her chin up. "Hey, this is me, remember? Tall, brown-eyed guy who keeps chickens? I couldn't have changed that much in five days."

A Freudian statement if she'd ever heard one . . . and one she didn't care to examine too closely. "You wouldn't think so," she said.

He stepped back, watching her, pushing his hands into the pockets of his slacks. "I knew this would come," he said conversationally. "I just didn't think it would be quite so soon." He gave her a quiet half-smile. "You've never been an easy lady to anticipate."

"I don't know what you're talking about."

"Sure you do. You just don't want to admit you know what I'm talking about. It's got you worried, hasn't it?"

Inside Stevie felt as spongy as the carpet beneath her toes. Her backbone seemed to have disappeared, and she couldn't get a handle on any one emotion. "What has me worried?"

"This," he said, gesturing around the room. "This luxury I've been wallowing in, and not a guinea hen to be seen. The fact that I've been going to board meetings instead of selling tents and mountain bikes. Your paranoia is creeping back, and you're wondering if I'm finally showing my true color. Blue, as in blood."

Stevie's stomach compressed into a tight knot, quicker to recognize the truth than she was. "I realize you're doing all this to help your father."

"And you're afraid I *like* it," he said, lowering his voice to a conspiratorial whisper. "Dr. Jekyll had Mr. Hyde controlling his soul, Mick Connover has—"

"You're acting like an idiot," Stevie muttered. She held his gaze for as long as she possibly could, then turned and walked to the windows. Not too close; even now she experienced the sensation of falling into space. "I could never sleep in this apartment," she said. "I'd be afraid I'd roll off my bed and tumble thirty stories to the ground."

He looked at her back, at the careful distance she kept between herself and the wall of glass. "You could probably sleep if you were as tired as I've been. My father was in the middle of a corporate buy-out when he had his attack. It's taken me twenty-five hours a day to close the deal."

She turned, her reflected gaze lifting to his. "Then the pressure's off?"

"Hopefully. I'm just playing this thing by ear until Marshall comes home and I can dump the whole mess in his lap. He'll love it. He thrives in a crisis."

"I see." She didn't move. She desperately wanted to salvage the evening, but didn't know how. There was nothing like a few home truths to throw a damper on a party.

"You had a haircut," she said abruptly. "I don't think I've ever seen your hair so . . . styled. It's very nice."

Immediately he raked his fingers through his hair, destroying any semblance of style. "Better?"

She smiled. "Better."

Better, but he could still sense a troubled desperation under the play. "We need to figure out what's gone wrong," he said.

"What do you mean?" It seemed to be her catchphrase tonight.

"Tonight. Our little dinner party is missing something." He frowned, then clicked his fingers together with sudden inspiration. "I know what it is. *Dinner.* We need sustenance. I have a half dozen cartons of Chinese food waiting in the oven. Sit at yonder table, ma'am. I'll fetch the vittles."

They sat opposite each other at the black lacquered table like negotiators at a labor dispute. The dark windows were hazy mirrors of disembodied furniture and glowing lamps. Stevie found herself staring at Mick's reflection in the glass, trying to find the man she felt comfortable with. She wished they were sitting next to each other. They looked so far apart in that long dark mirror.

The phone rang just as they were finishing their meal. Mick excused himself and took the call in the kitchen. Stevie broke open her fortune cookie and read it aloud to an empty room: "Hold Your Tongue Unless You Can Improve the Silence."

Mick came back into the room, shrugging into a suit coat. "I'm sorry Stevie, but I have to leave you for a few minutes. That was one of our accountants downstairs. He's been working late on some figures I need for a board meeting in the morning. If I don't look them over, I'm going to sound as uninformed as I really am."

Stevie crumpled up her fortune and tossed it over her shoulder. "Don't apologize. First things come first."

Their gazes held for a long moment—his

watchful, hers purposely blank. "I won't be long," he said. "Please wait."

"No." Stevie pushed her chair back and stood up. "I have a big day tomorrow. We're giving a surprise party for the manager of a restaurant in Newport Beach. I still have some loose ends to tie up."

"You sure do," Mick said tonelessly. "And they're right here. Don't you dare walk out on me, sweet cakes."

"I'm not the only one walking out," she replied casually. She went to the sofa, slipped on her shoes and picked up her purse. She was inanimate, deaf to the inner voice that told her she was making a mistake. "I understand you're preoccupied with business right now. I don't want to put any more pressure on you than you already have. Why don't you call me when Marshall comes home and things get back to normal?"

Mick came up behind her, his hand gripping her arm, turning her to face him. "Why don't you wait for me here for ten bloody minutes?"

Silence vibrated between them.

"Sometimes it's just better to let things go," Stevie said tightly. Her eyes felt painfully dry, as if begging for the moisture that tears would bring. "Tonight's just a bad night. We both need some time, that's all."

Mick let her go, acknowledging defeat with an exasperated breath. "You could be right," he said softly, each word arriving with individual intensity. "Maybe we do need some time. One of us sure as hell needs to do some heavy thinking. I defer to your wisdom, Stevie." He brushed past her and opened the door. "After you."

They shared the elevator in thick silence. Mick leaned one hip against the wall, studying Stevie with heavy-lidded eyes. Stevie stared at the instrument panel as if it were a picture window.

Mick stopped the elevator at the sixth floor. "This is where I get off." Then, when Stevie opened her mouth to say good-bye, he raised his hand, silencing her abruptly. "Don't you dare," he said softly. "Don't you *dare*."

Chapter
10

"I KNEW HE WAS guilty. He had these little pig eyes smashed way down in his face, watery blue pig eyes. The first time I saw him, I knew. I can tell you, though, it took some time for the other jurors to see through the guy. Just because he was a doctor, they couldn't believe he was capable of such a heinous crime."

"Hold it," Morgan said. "What's heinous?"

Marcy the receptionist was back from two weeks of jury duty. She was relating her thrilling experience to Stevie and Morgan over a tuna sandwich in Stevie's office. "Heinous means... depraved."

"*That* word he's familiar with," Stevie murmured.

"Anyway," Marcy said, "apparently this guy

was totally whacked out. Nuts. It was bad enough that he killed his father-in-law, but to try and frame his mother-in-law—"

"Someone's in the outside office," Stevie said. "I heard the door."

"Oh. Well, I need to get back to work, anyway." Marcy gathered up her used baggies and paper lunch bag from Stevie's desk. "I'll see who it is. Remind me to tell you guys about the slides they showed us. They were incredible. I tell you, I will never again see a fireplace poker without remembering—"

"See who's in the front office," Stevie said faintly. Her fragile stomach reminded her never to be called for jury duty.

"Fascinating story," Morgan said when Marcy had gone. "I'll bet you enjoyed it immensely. It was morbid and depressing, which kind of fits the mood you've been in the past couple of weeks."

"Don't start on me, Morgan. Not this time."

Morgan's sandy brows shot up. "Start on you? What ever could you mean? I'm simply being observant."

"Fine. Go be observant in your own office."

"I shall," he said kindly, "after I offer a pearl of wisdom: 'If happiness truly consisted of physical ease and freedom from care, the happiest individual would be the American cow.'"

Stevie stared at him. "Thank you, Morgan," she said tonelessly.

The door opened just enough for Marcy's curly red head. "You have a visitor, Stevie. Tamara Connover. Should I send her in?"

Tamara. Stevie hadn't been expecting her. As a matter of fact, she hadn't even known she was back from her honeymoon. It had been nearly two weeks since she'd left Mick at the sixth floor of the Connover Building without a good-bye. Since then, the telephone had been ominously silent. True to his word, Mick was giving her time to think. Very possibly a lifetime. "Show her in," she said. Then, to Morgan, "Show yourself out."

"I know when I'm not wanted," Morgan said. "And I'm proud to say it isn't often." He passed Tamara going out the door, giving her a wave and a jaunty smile. "A honeymoon looks good on you, Tamara. That's one gorgeous tan."

Tamara sailed into the room on a cloud of expensive perfume, giving Stevie a brief hug. "Hello, darling! I'm back and I have a gorgeous tan, or so says your handsome friend. I know I met him at the reception, but I can't remember his name."

"Morgan," Stevie said, "and he's not my friend. He's my cross to bear. Now sit down and tell me about your trip."

Tamara sat in the chair Marcy had recently vacated and folded her hands demurely in her lap. With her choirboy haircut and absurdly pert nose, she was the very fabric of charming Americana. "I will not tell you all about my honeymoon. I would blush. I will, however, tell you that I am a happy woman. Which is not what I came by to tell you."

Stevie shook her head slowly. "Run that by me again, please."

"I just wanted to tell you how happy I am for you and Mick. And stunned. Darling, you could have knocked me over with a feather when Mick told me the news. I mean, of all people in the world for you to get involved with—"

Stevie's mind seemed to jump into a new state of wakefulness. "What news?"

"You *know* what news. He said you were going to live with him forever on his mountain. You can imagine how surprised I was. I know how you feel about the almighty dollar. I thought you were going to shun me forever when I fell in love with Marshall. Heavens, when I think of the times I tried to persuade you to come to this party or that party to meet him—"

"He said we were going to live together?"

Tamara nodded, brown hair swinging. "His exact words were, 'We're going to live in the little adobe thing forever and have fresh flowers on the table every day.' I wouldn't count on the flowers, the man is hell on foliage. Anyway, when Mick first asked me about you, I thought, Ohmigosh, he hasn't got a prayer. But then I thought how lovely the two of you would be together, and I encouraged him. I'm so happy I was right."

"But you weren't," Stevie said blankly. "I mean, you were, but... Tamara, when your father-in-law had his heart attack and Mick went to work for the company—"

"Oh, I know all that." Tamara waved her hand in the air. "Mick told me."

With every startled pop of her heart, Stevie could feel herself growing fainter. "He told you?" she parroted weakly.

"Well . . . yes. He said you were still a little paranoid when it came to three-piece suits. But then he just smiled and said you were never going to say good-bye to each other, so you'd have to trust him eventually. He has a wonderful smile, doesn't he?" she added reflectively. "Almost as sexy as Marshall's. Ohmigosh, Marshall!" She looked at her watch, then rolled her eyes to the ceiling. "I was supposed to meet him for lunch fifteen minutes ago. Look, I wanted to see if the four of us could get together sometime, maybe for dinner. What do you think?"

"I think . . ." What did she think? About Mick, constantly. About the little adobe thing and the flowers she'd promised to water. About her own insecurities and her itty-bitty tendency to overreact when it came to certain things. Softly she whispered, "I think I better start today."

"Start? Start what?"

"Never saying good-bye."

Mick drove home slowly that afternoon. He couldn't think of a single reason to hurry. His garden was doing poorly, and would continue to do poorly regardless of the care he gave it. His house was empty, and it looked as if it would continue to be empty for some time to come. It was difficult to be excited about an anemic garden and a lonely house.

Ah well, he told himself. The chickens needed to be fed. They would be happy to see him.

He pulled into his drive and nearly rear-ended a little blue car. Stevie's little blue car.

He sat in the Jeep for several minutes, trying to calm his poor leaping heart. He'd imagined this so many times. He'd waited and he'd wished, and she'd been there, inside every one of those wishes. He looked down at his clothes. Damn. His shirt had a smear of grease on the front from a mountain bike he'd repaired that morning. Smack-dab across his stomach. He looked into the rearview mirror and tried to do something with his windblown hair, only to find nothing could be done. Oh, well. She liked messy hair.

Stevie.

Walking up the sidewalk, he noticed the flowers had been watered. Was it his imagination, or did they already look a little healthier? Certainly the daisies had perked up.

It took his eyes a moment to become adjusted to the interior shadows of the house. Everything seemed terribly quiet. He looked in the living room and bedroom and found them empty, and his heart skipped nervously into his throat. He looked in the kitchen and saw a vase of fresh flowers on the table, and he sighed and smiled to himself. They weren't from his garden. They were beautiful. He pulled a long-stemmed rose from the vase, a thorn spearing his finger. He didn't even feel it.

Carrying the rose, he went out the back door, shading his eyes as he surveyed his domain. Dumbo Williams' stubby little body was barely visible at the far end of the pasture, yet even from this distance, he could see his huge ears flopping. His chickens were scratching contentedly in the coop. His vegetable garden, like his flowers, had recently been watered.

And Stevie Knight was reclining on her stomach in the shade of an avocado tree. She wore short shorts and his very own T-shirt. Her long legs were deliciously tanned, bent at the knees and crossed in midair at the ankles. She was writing something on a tablet of paper, her brow furrowed with the most endearing expression of absolute concentration.

She looked so good to him, so beautiful. Time stopped, giving him a perfectly beautiful moment of his own. There was nothing but the sun beating down from the bleached blue sky and the sound of his own heart in his ears. And the woman who looked at him now with softly parted lips and her love in her eyes.

"I heard the Jeep," she said. "What took you so long?"

"I've been looking for you. Under tables and chairs, things like that." He sat down beside her and offered the rose with charming solemnity. "For you. I promised you fresh flowers every day."

Her wide mouth tipped in a soft smile. "It looks kind of familiar."

"I didn't know I was having a visitor," he said. "I had to improvise. What are you writing?"

"I'm not writing." She sat up, tucking her knees beneath her, lifting the pad of paper for him to see. "I'm drawing a portrait. Do you like it?"

It was a little stick horse standing in a fenced pasture. His ears were nearly the size of his little stick legs. "It's beautiful," Mick pronounced. "Dumbo has never looked so good."

"Actually, he wasn't the subject I had in mind when I drove up here," she confided. "I had something more...two-legged...in mind." Mick looked pointedly at the chickens, and she shook her head. "No, I want some real inspiration. A flesh and blood man."

"I'm flesh," Mick said. He showed her his pricked finger. "And I'm blood. Will I do?"

"Well, that depends." Her voice was languid, her fingers gently tracing the curling petals of the rose. "You would have to be a very patient subject."

His eyes never left her face, though he lifted a hand and tucked the burnished fall of her hair behind one ear. "I'm awfully patient," he said huskily, thinking of the past two weeks.

"I'm just a beginner." She lifted the flower, brushing the exquisite red silk across her lips. "It could take me a very long time to capture the real you. Days, weeks, years even. I wouldn't want to be any trouble."

"I haven't got anything special planned for the rest of my life," he said, envying the rose. "So it wouldn't be any trouble, really. You could take as long as you'd like."

Her voice came again, softly caressing him. "I probably should mention that I'm not a very patient person. And sometimes I act before I think. And I've been known to be a little insecure at times. You'd have to be very tolerant and forgiving."

"I can live with that," Mick said. He leaned forward and pressed his lips into her hair, feeling it slide against his flesh like some weightless silken textile. "As a matter of fact . . . I don't think I can live without it."

Very carefully she put the rose down on the tablet of paper in her lap, then lifted the tablet to the grass. The light in her eyes became a warm glow as she studied his face. She touched her fingertips to the heat stain in his cheeks, then moved closer, placing soft kisses along his jaw and chin, finally settling on his lips. Between the slow, open-mouthed kisses she was pressing there, she whispered, "So I can . . . stay here . . . on your mountain?"

"Oh, yes." His breath was painful in his throat and his blood felt like it was ninety-percent oxygen: rich, rushing through his head, singing in his pulses. "You can stay forever."

Grasping his wrists, she led them to her

breasts, stirring them against the soft fabric of his T-shirt. "Then we won't ever have to say good-bye."

"Never, ever." His voice was breathless and hoarse, as if he'd been running a long time. His hands massaged in widening circles, working and molding the tender flesh. He was heated everywhere, the surface of his skin flushed and stinging, a deeper warmth building in the pit of his stomach. "I knew you'd come home. I knew if I waited, and I believed long enough, you'd come home to me . . ."

Home. Her thoughts were a restless blur, but that sweet word touched her with quiet intensity. She gazed into his feverish eyes, framing his beloved face in her trembling hands, loving him with all her heart, all her soul. Her lashes sparkled with her own tears, soothing his hot skin as he kissed her with reverence, with hunger. She was dancing in sunlight, she was drifting in a star-studded night.

She was home.

Outside Mick's open window the sky had turned to the deep lustre of a dark cherry. The soft, dying day crept into the bedroom, spilling red and gold on the tumbled covers. Mick and Stevie admired the sunset, her head nestled against his shoulder, his hands playing absently in her hair.

"I have your present," he said suddenly. "I forgot about it."

"What present?" Stevie asked.

"Belated birthday present." He turned on his side, reaching beneath the bed. "Here it is."

She started to cry the moment she looked at the package. It was wrapped in pink and white paper, and tied with a very pretty white bow. One end of the ribbon was curled, the other was shredded in an obvious attempt to curl it.

Still sniffing, she opened the box. There it was, framed and matted like any fine piece of art work. A stick figure with Orphan Annie eyes and corkscrew curls, standing beneath an oblong sun. "My picture," she said softly, touching the artist's signature at the bottom with her fingers.

"Sweet Cakes," by M. J. Connover

He smiled with his incredibly sexy mouth. "Just a reminder that no one will ever see you quite the way I do."

"I knew that the first moment I kidnapped you."

From the <u>New York Times</u> bestselling author
of <u>Morning Glory</u>

LaVyrle Spencer

One of today's best-loved authors
of bittersweet human drama and
captivating romance.

<u>New York Times</u> bestselling
author
CYNTHIA FREEMAN

Cynthia Freeman is one of today's best-loved authors of bittersweet human drama and captivating love stories.

___ILLUSIONS OF LOVE	0-425-08529-5/$4.50
___SEASONS OF THE HEART	0-425-09557-6/$4.50
___THE LAST PRINCESS	0-425-11601-8/$4.95